A LIGHT IN THE CASTLE

THE YOUNG UNDERGROUND

A LIGHT IN THE CASTLE

Robert Elmer

BETHANY HOUSE PUBLISHERS
MINNEAPOLIS, MINNESOTA 55438

Published by Bethany House Publishers
A Ministry of Bethany Fellowship, Inc.
11300 Hampshire Avenue South
Minneapolis, Minnesota 55438

Printed in the United States of America.

Library of Congress Cataloging-in-Publication Data

Elmer, Robert.
    A light in the castle / Robert Elmer.
        p.   cm. — (The young underground ; 6)
    Summary: In 1945, while taking a train to Copenhagen to meet the king, Peter and Elise meet a man with a strange clocklike device and later have other strange adventures and encounters.
    ISBN 1–55661–659–7 (pbk.)
    [1. Denmark—Fiction. 2. Brothers and sisters—Fiction. 3. Christian life—Fiction. 4. Mystery and detective stories.] I. Title. II. Series: Elmer, Robert. Young underground ; #6.
PZ7.E4794Li   1996
[Fic]—dc20

                                                        96–25297
                                                        CIP
                                                        AC

To Stefan Peter—
who makes us smile.

ROBERT ELMER has written and edited numerous articles for both newspapers and magazines in the Pacific Northwest. THE YOUNG UNDERGROUND series was inspired by stories from Robert's Denmark-born parents, as well as friends who lived through the years of German occupation. He is currently a writer for an advertising agency in Bellingham, Washington. He and his wife, Ronda, have three children.

CONTENTS

CELEBRITIES

"I'll get it!" Peter and Elise Andersen shouted a duet as they raced for the telephone.

"My turn to answer the phone this time!" insisted Peter. He was a little smaller than his twelve-year-old twin sister, but they both had the same deep blue eyes, medium blond hair, and lanky build. He did his best to beat her to the phone, scrambling over a kitchen chair.

"Don't bother, little brother." Elise was already two steps ahead. She scooped up the receiver, flipped her shoulder-length hair, and smiled sweetly in his direction.

"Andersen residence, Elise speaking."

Peter made a face at her and tried to get close to hear who was calling, but she only batted him away.

"Yes, this is the same Elise. Well, yes, we have had a few reporters ask us questions. An interview? Sure, but I'd better ask my mother. Peter? Oh, sure, I guess he can talk to you while I talk to Mom. I'll be right back. Here he is."

Elise pointed at Peter, but he only wrinkled his brow at her.

"Who is it?" he whispered.

She pushed the receiver at him and mouthed the words "newspaper reporter" before running down the hall to find their mom.

"Uh, hullo?" Peter croaked.

"Hi, Peter" came the voice of a fast-talking man. "Your sister said you'd be glad to talk to me for a minute, since you're a celebrity. Could you tell me what it was like to escape from a German submarine? I'd like to do an article on the two of you."

"Uh, yeah, sure. Who is this?" Peter felt his palms sweating.

"I'm sorry, I didn't introduce myself. Finn Ipsen, reporter for *The Times*, down in Copenhagen. We want to do a full interview with you and your sister, plus your parents, if we can. Tell the whole country how you and Elise and . . . what was his name?"

"Henrik. My friend Henrik."

"Right. How you and Elise and Henrik stowed away on the German submarine and saved the art treasures of Europe. Incredible story."

"Uh, sure. Well . . ."

"We want to get a better angle, though. I've read the articles in the other papers, even the one in your own city, but you never really explained how you made it through that adventure."

"Uh . . ." Peter shifted from foot to foot, trying to think of what to say.

"Let me ask you another way, Peter," the rapid-fire reporter continued. "How did you manage to escape?"

"Escape. Yeah, well, we were pretty lucky."

"Luck? That's how you explain it?"

Peter looked up to see his pretty, red-haired mother standing in front of him with her hands on her hips. It was a sure sign that he had better hand over the phone.

"Uh, listen," began Peter. "I'd love to talk with you some more, but my mom is here now. Here she is."

Peter breathed a sigh of relief and held the phone out to his mother.

"Karen Andersen here. I'm Peter and Elise's mother."

Peter's mother didn't look pleased to talk to the reporter, but she politely answered a couple of questions.

"Yes, sure, that would be fine. The kids will be excited to talk to a reporter from *The Times*, although they've had quite a lot of excitement already. You'll take the train here from Copenhagen? Tomorrow morning, then, at ten. The address is 54 Axeltorv Street, second floor, next to Clausen's Bakery. Not hard to find, Mr. Ipsen. Fine. Goodbye."

Peter and Elise hovered over their mother as she hung up the phone. She was a petite woman, not much bigger than her two children.

"This one sounds even pushier than the last two reporters," she told them, then she shook her head and shrugged. "But I suppose it's not every day that three twelve-year-olds are kidnapped on a German submarine. I just wish it could have been someone else."

"Oh, Mom," said Elise. "You don't need to worry about us."

"I'm not worried now. Not like I was before, when you kids disappeared and we didn't know . . ."

She paused, tears filling her eyes.

"Mom, are you okay?" asked Elise, putting a hand on her mother's shoulder.

Mrs. Andersen cleared her throat and forced a smile. "I'm fine now. It's just all these reporters. All those headlines."

"Yeah," said Peter, remembering some of the articles that had already been written about them. "Like 'Twelve-Year-Old Heroes.'" Peter had clipped that article and sent it to Henrik in Sweden, after his friend had rushed off to see his sick father, who still couldn't be moved home.

"Or 'Three Kids Save Europe's Art Treasures,'" continued their mother.

"I don't know why they said that," Elise wondered aloud. "They weren't really art treasures, except for the crown jewels."

Peter nodded and sat down at the kitchen table with his

mother. "My favorite was the one that said 'Twins Fish Millions From Sub.'"

"It's not so bad, Mom," Elise tried to tell her mother, who was pacing back and forth. Mrs. Andersen didn't look convinced.

"The only bad part," said Peter, "is that Henrik is missing out on everything again. After all we went through together in the submarine."

"I don't think he's missing out on too much," his mother told him. "But I am concerned about his father." She reached over and put her hand on Peter's shoulder. Peter rested his chin in one hand and nodded. He knew Henrik's father wasn't expected to live much longer, not after his heart attacks. But as usual, Peter's best friend had been cheerfully telling jokes as he left on the ferry back to Sweden the week before.

"It's a shame the Melchiors haven't been able to come home to Denmark since they escaped," mused their mother, a faraway look in her dark eyes. "Their home is waiting for them."

Their conversation was interrupted by the sound of someone coming up the steps from the street below. Tonight the steps sounded a little quicker, though, and Peter looked up eagerly to see his tall, wide-shouldered father stride in through the living room door.

"I'm home!" Mr. Andersen whistled cheerily as he slipped his worn black leather briefcase next to the kitchen table, the way he always did. He tossed a stack of mail down onto the table between two plates. "How come no one picked up the mail today?"

"Oh, Arne, we must have forgotten," answered Mrs. Andersen, standing up to greet her husband. "With all the excitement today . . ."

"Pretty tough business, being the national heroes, huh?"

Peter ducked as his father tried to muss his hair.

"Guess what we're doing tomorrow, Dad," Peter challenged his father.

Mr. Andersen gave his son a puzzled glance as he walked to the stove to inspect dinner. The steam from a pot of boiled potatoes hit him in the face when he lifted the lid.

"How did you know?" asked Mr. Andersen, pulling away from the stove. "I haven't said anything yet."

"What are you talking about, Arne?" asked Mrs. Andersen, shooing him away so she could check on the cabbage.

"Well, it wouldn't exactly be a vacation. But Mr. Haugland at the bank was supposed to go to a four-day conference in Copenhagen, and he came down with some kind of flu last night. Now he wants me to go instead. So how about we *all* go for a week to Copenhagen?"

"Oh," sighed Mrs. Andersen. "It would be wonderful to escape all these news reporters. The phone has been ringing off the hook."

"So when do we leave?" Peter was ready to travel. "We hardly ever get to go to Copenhagen—not to do the fun stuff."

"Tomorrow morning early," replied Mr. Andersen, taking off his steamy glasses and rubbing his eyes. "My first meeting starts at ten-thirty."

"Oh!" exclaimed Mrs. Andersen. "But—"

"But, Dad," complained Elise. "That's what we were going to tell you. Another newspaper reporter is coming at ten to interview us. From *The Times*. We can't leave that early."

"And a photographer even," added Peter.

Mr. Andersen sat down to his place at the kitchen table. "Well, then, you'll have to take a later train and I'll meet you at the station. They haven't told me where we're staying yet, anyway."

As Mr. Andersen sat in the kitchen talking with their mother, Peter started to pick up their mail, but his frisky cat Tiger beat him to one envelope that had slipped under the table. Tiger batted at the envelope and caught it in his claw as if it were a mouse.

"Hey, you, give me that envelope!" protested Peter.

"If it's another bill, tell your cat he can have it for dinner," joked their father.

Peter dived under the table and grabbed the letter from Tiger's playful grip, then stopped for a look. He turned the plain white envelope over and over again, wanting to be sure.

"Peter, come out from under the table," ordered Mrs. Andersen. "It's time to wash up."

Peter looked at the return address one more time to make sure his eyes weren't playing tricks.

"Mom, you won't believe this," he told them, still under the table. He backed out carefully and straightened up.

"It's a letter from the king, and it's addressed to me and Elise!"

"Let me see," said Elise, trying to grab the letter. But Peter held it out of her reach and just showed her the return address.

"It's not a joke, Dad," she gasped, looking at the official gold-imprinted stationery.

Mrs. Andersen wiped her hands on her apron and came over to where the twins were sitting on the floor. "What are you two talking about? Here, stand up and let us all see this."

Peter read the letter out loud so they could all hear. "It says at the top, 'King Christian the Tenth,' and it has his royal seal, the one with the crown and the C and the X."

"We can see that," insisted Elise. "So read it."

Peter cleared his throat, feeling important. "Okay. 'July 12, 1945.' That was last week. '54 Axeltorv Street, Helsingor. Dear Peter and Elise . . .'" He checked to see if Elise would interrupt him or try to read it faster than he could. She made impatient windmill circles with both hands but said nothing.

" 'Having read the recent newspaper account of your adventures on the German submarine, I would be most pleased to hear of your stories in person. If your schedules permit, please join me for tea at two on the afternoon of Thursday, July 19, at the Royal Amalienborg Palace. Your parents, of course, would be most welcome, as well.' And then it's signed, 'King Christian the Tenth of Denmark.' "

The twins' parents were silent for a long moment, and then Mrs. Andersen sat down at the kitchen table with a sigh.

"As I was telling you, Arne," she said, "this has been quite a day."

———

"Can you believe it, Elise?" Peter talked to the door of the bathroom after dinner as his sister was brushing her teeth. From inside she just mumbled.

"First all the newspaper reporters," he continued, counting off the events on his hand. "Then the guy from *The Times* calls, then Dad says we're going to Copenhagen, and now the king wants to meet us!"

"Wake me up when it's over," agreed Elise.

Still feeling in a daze, Peter wandered down the hall until he came upon Tiger. The cat was batting around a little ball of tangled yarn.

"Here, boy." Peter got down on his knees next to Tiger and rolled the yarn for him to chase. "Let me tell you about where we're going. Too bad you can't come with us. Grandpa is going to have to take care of you while we're gone."

The cat looked up at him with his typical "I don't care, keep playing with me!" expression. Peter smiled and chased the ball with the cat into the living room, where Mr. Andersen was reading the paper. The cat batted the ball toward Peter, Peter batted it back, and Tiger jumped straight up into the air. They both landed in a heap, Peter laughing the whole time.

THE MAN ON
THE TRAIN

"Do you have the invitation, Peter?" asked Elise.

Little Danish towns with white churches and tile roofs flew by their train window, but his twin sister didn't seem to notice.

"Right here." Peter patted the back pocket where he had been keeping the invitation from the king they had received the day before.

"I'm so glad that we were able to escape all the phone calls," said Mrs. Andersen. "Are you sure all this hasn't been too much for you two?"

"Too much?" Peter gave his mother a puzzled look.

Mrs. Andersen laughed. "Okay, okay, so you're stuck with being famous. But now we're on vacation, don't forget."

Elise unfolded her long legs and stood up, like a cat waking up from a nap. "We won't forget, Mom. But can we take a walk before we get to the city?"

Mrs. Andersen looked up and down the aisle. Most of the people in the train were either sitting at their high-backed brown seats, reading, trying to sleep, or chatting quietly. The aisle was clear.

"Only for a few minutes. And stay together. We don't have that much longer to go."

Peter eagerly stepped out into the aisle, followed by his sister.

"You're going to lose that invitation, Peter," Elise warned him. "It's hanging halfway out of your pocket."

"It's fine," answered Peter, checking the invitation.

"You'd better make sure it is. Listen, I've been thinking. . . ."

Uh-oh, thought Peter. *I'm not sure I like the way that sounds.*

"Yeah?" he asked. "About what?"

"Well, do you think you said the right thing to *The Times* reporter we talked to this morning? You didn't really explain things."

Peter stepped around the feet of a sleeping man. By then he knew what his sister was going to say, and he knew she would be right. But to admit it now . . .

"What's wrong with what I said?" he answered, a little defensively.

Elise frowned, then pretended to hold a notebook and a pen.

"So, tell me, Peter," she said in a husky voice, imitating the reporter. "How did you get away from the German submarine out in the middle of the ocean?"

Then she imitated Peter, turning her head the other way. "Oh, I don't know," she said, scratching her head. "We were just lucky, I guess."

"But did you pray or anything?" she continued, using the reporter voice.

"Um, let me see. . . ." She switched over once more to the Peter imitation and put her hands up with a shrug. "Not that I remember. Besides, I'm too embarrassed to tell you, even if I did."

Peter waved his hand at his blond-haired sister as if he were swatting a fly and continued down the aisle. "That's not the way it was, Elise. I didn't say that."

"Yeah, but that's the way it came across," she answered, back to her normal voice. "And you know what I think? I think you're so thrilled about seeing our pictures in the newspaper that you've forgotten what went on. You didn't say anything about what *really* happened."

Peter crossed his arms. "Okay, so what was I supposed to say?"

"You know exactly what I mean."

Peter reached for the sliding door into the next car and pulled hard. "I don't want to argue with you anymore, Elise. Seems like that's all we've been doing since we got back."

They stepped into the space between the train cars, and when Peter looked down he could see the blur of the tracks speeding by. He stopped for a moment, feeling a rush of wind. He caught the eye-watering, gritty smell of the train's engine up ahead.

"Hurry up," Elise urged him with a nudge. "I don't want to fall through."

"Okay, when we get to the next car," Peter called back over the sound of the tracks, "let's try to figure out who people are just by looking at them."

Once in the next car, Peter and Elise took their time strolling down the aisle.

"That guy in the back corner is a bank robber," whispered Peter, pointing with his eyes to a man with a dark hat, reading a newspaper.

"How do you know?" Elise whispered back.

Peter shrugged. "Some things you can just tell." They continued down the corridor to the next car. "Take the lady who was sitting next to the door at the end of the car . . ."

"The one with all that bright red makeup?"

"Right. She's really a circus performer. Does the high wire."

Elise finally giggled, which is what Peter had hoped for.

"And the guy coming toward us?" Elise whispered into Peter's ear. "Is that a spy?"

Peter looked up in time to see a short, unshaven man with scuffed shoes and torn brown trousers trying to slip by them. His eyebrows were as bushy as black caterpillars, and he was carrying a heavy travel bag—something like an old-fashioned doctor's bag that opened at the top. The corner of the bag caught Peter squarely in the shin.

"Ow!" yelped Peter, more in surprise than pain. The train jolted over an uneven set of tracks, and Peter fell backward into the man. Grabbing for a handhold, Peter caught the top of the man's bag, sending it flying. Elise tried to catch the bag, but it flipped over, spilling its contents all over the aisle.

Instantly the pudgy little man pounced on his luggage, trying to cover everything by almost lying on it. Without a word he stuffed wires and switches and other electrical parts back into his bag. Peter and Elise got down on their knees to help.

"Sorry, sir," said Peter, reaching for a bundle of small wires. "Can we help you pick all this up?"

"*Nein!*" hissed the man, his eyes wild like a mother panther guarding her young. Then he seemed to catch himself, but he didn't stop moving. "I mean, no, thank you."

The ferocious look on the man's unshaved face made Peter and Elise both back up in fright, get to their feet, and hurry away.

"That guy was weird," whispered Elise, shuddering.

"And did you hear what he said?" Peter looked back quickly over his shoulder to see if anyone was coming their way. Already the man was gone. "I thought I heard him say 'Nein.' That sounded German to me."

Elise shook her head. "I don't know, Peter. I thought it sounded like Danish. Here, the conductor is coming this way. We'd better go sit down again."

"Arriving in Copenhagen, five minutes," announced the silver-haired man who had taken their tickets earlier in the trip. He wore a black uniform and visored cap.

The twins turned around and hurried past the place where the man with the travel bag had bumped into them. The train lurched again, and Elise stopped for a moment to pick something up off the floor.

"What are you doing?" asked Peter as Elise bent over. She

turned around with an object in her hand that looked like a small silver-plated alarm clock.

"Look at this," she said, turning it over. "Do you think it came out of that man's little black bag?"

"It looks like something he dropped," replied Peter, looking closely at the instrument. There was no one sitting in several rows of that section of the train—except an older woman wearing a fur shawl and a hat with fluffy white feathers. Elise stepped over to the woman.

"Uh, excuse me," Elise said, holding up the clock, or timer, or whatever it was. "You didn't drop this on the floor, did you?"

The woman looked over her silver wire-frame glasses at Elise and wrinkled her nose doubtfully. "I should say not. But perhaps it belongs to that man who spilled all his belongings here a few moments ago."

"Thanks." Elise continued on toward the door. "That's what I thought."

"But what is it?" asked Peter. "It's not an alarm clock."

"Maybe we can find him and give it back," said Elise as they returned to their seats.

"Are you kidding?" asked Peter. "He's a spy! And you should have smelled his breath!"

"Peter!" scolded Elise. "He's no such thing. If this belongs to him, we need to return it."

She pushed open the door to the next car and almost ran straight into the man they had been looking for. They all stood there in the noisy space between the two cars, and then he tried to move around them.

"Excuse me." Elise cleared her throat and spoke as loudly as she could above the noise of the tracks below. She held up the timer. "Did you lose this when you dropped your bag?"

The man's eyes took on almost the same flame as they had before, and his caterpillar eyebrows danced.

"You kids!" he snarled, grabbing at Elise's wrist. The timer fell from her hand and wedged into a corner, while she stepped sideways. The train shook once more, throwing Elise off balance. As she began to fall Peter reached for her arm, but her foot slipped through a large crack between the cars, and she fell to her knee.

"Peter!" she gasped as Peter reached down to help her up.

The man's expression changed from anger to surprise, and he tried to help as well.

"Hey," he said. "I didn't mean for you to fall down."

Peter could hear the grinding of the train wheels as they made a corner, and he tried desperately to pull Elise up. If they turned the corner the other way, the small space between the cars would close up and snap Elise's leg like a toothpick.

"My leg is stuck!" she told him, panic on her face.

"What do you mean, it's stuck?"

"I mean my shoe! Something's caught on my shoe."

Peter looked up to see the uncertain look on the man's face.

"Grab that shoulder," commanded Peter. "I'll get this one."

The train started to turn. Peter knew they had to pull Elise out in the next few seconds, or . . .

"Pull!" cried Peter, locking his hands under Elise's arm. He tugged and leaned back as hard as he could.

At first nothing happened, but then Elise pushed with her free leg. A second later she popped up like a piece of toast from a toaster and fell back on top of Peter. The train kept turning, and Peter looked down to see the opening snap shut.

"There now," said the man, dusting himself off. Peter could tell he had an accent of some sort, but he wasn't sure what kind. The man picked up his timer and stuffed it into his bag, then turned to the twins with a huge, phony smile. Sweat beaded on his pink forehead. "No harm done, eh?"

Neither of them knew what to say after their bizarre tug-of-war. Peter just wanted to get away from this strange little man.

"Now look . . ." The man pulled out a billfold from his back pocket, picked out a wad of money, and thrust a bill at Elise. "I'm grateful that you returned my . . . uh . . . piece of science—uh, test equipment."

Peter shook his head and tried to reach for the door to get back to their compartment.

"No," the twins said at almost the same time.

"Thanks anyway," mumbled Peter. "But you should keep your money."

"No, I insist." The man's twisted smile never left his lips. Peter looked down at the money—fifty crowns! That was enough for a bicycle, or a shortwave radio, or maybe both. He hadn't seen that much money in a long time.

"Yes, take it," insisted the man. "I wouldn't have been able to do my science experiments here if it weren't for you two children. Saves me a long trip back to, uh, Poland. Take it, please, and then there will be no reason for you to repeat anything about this little accident. This is quite confidential, you see. . . ."

That was it. Peter realized the man wasn't offering them a reward, but a bribe to be quiet. But why? Elise tried for the door, too, but another man stepped through and stopped.

"Rolf?" said the man. Taller and gray-haired, he looked like a retired wrestler. Peter thought he saw a tattoo of some kind on the man's forearm, just under the sleeve of his shirt. But the little man said nothing, only held the wrestler back with his hand.

"My dear children, think of what you can do with fifty crowns. Shall we say fifty crowns apiece? Tell your mother you found it on the floor, if you like. In fact, that would be a very good idea if you did, yes."

Peter didn't wait to hear any more. In one quick movement he ducked past the wrestler, who didn't seem to know what was happening.

"Excuse us," said Elise, stepping on the back of Peter's shoe.

The man growled again as they brushed by, but he didn't try to grab them. Peter didn't look back until they were well inside the next train car. All he could see through the window in the door was the little man looking curiously at an envelope.

The invitation! Peter felt for the invitation from the king in his back pocket. Gone.

"Elise, I dropped the invitation," he told his sister, but she didn't seem to hear him as she made her way up the aisle to their seats.

Peter looked back once more, and Mr. Eyebrows was holding the invitation and looking his direction with a funny half-grin on his face. A chill ran up Peter's spine, and he turned and ran back to his seat.

There's no way I'm going to go back there and claim it, thought Peter.

Their mother looked up from her magazine. "Oh, there you are, kids. I'm glad you're back. We're almost to the city."

Both of them were breathing hard, and their mother raised her eyebrow. "You haven't been running up and down the aisles, have you?"

Peter shook his head. "Mom, there was this guy—"

Suddenly Mrs. Andersen noticed Elise's left foot, the one with just a sock.

"Elise Andersen! Whatever happened to your shoe? And your leg's all dirty. It looks like something Peter would have done."

"We found this thing," she told her mother, still trying to catch her breath. "It looked like a clock, only smaller."

She tried to explain what had happened, but the conductor came back through the aisle just then, looking at the watch on his chain. "Arriving Copenhagen," he bellowed as he hurried down the aisle.

Peter looked out the window, watching the buildings go by as they neared the city. They went through a couple of tunnels, getting closer to a place Peter remembered from a few months earlier, before the war had ended. Only that had not been a vacation at all, and Peter tried to put the wartime out of his mind.

That was a long time ago, he told himself, fighting back the memory of when they had to escape from the Germans by running through those same railroad tunnels with his Uncle Morten and Lisbeth von Schreider. Actually, she was now Lisbeth Andersen, since the wedding almost two months earlier.

"We should tell the conductor," suggested Peter.

"What do we tell him?" said Elise. "That a Polish man made me fall and lose my shoe? I'm okay."

"But, Mom," said Peter. "Elise didn't tell you that the Mr. Eyebrows guy tried to make us not tell. He tried to give us money, even. Fifty crowns each, like it was some kind of big deal."

Mrs. Andersen's face clouded over in anger. "And you took it?"

"Of course not, Mom," answered Elise, sounding defensive.

"Well! The nerve of a strange man. What didn't he want you to tell?"

"That's what we can't figure out," explained Elise. "All we did was find that clock thing of his."

"Yeah," agreed Peter. "We were trying to be nice and give it back to him. I wasn't sure, but Elise thought it would be the right thing to do."

"And then this other man came, this taller man, with a tattoo. . . ." Elise's lip quivered as she told the story, and she wiped her eye with her sleeve. Peter even added the part about losing the king's invitation.

"Peter, I told you—" Elise's tears suddenly turned to anger at her brother's carelessness.

"Never mind, Elise." Mrs. Andersen got to her feet. Her cheeks had turned almost as red as her shoulder-length hair. "You find another pair of shoes in your suitcase. I'm going to go have a word with this character, whoever he is."

But just as Mrs. Andersen got to her feet, she had to reach out to keep her balance. The train slowed, bumped, and turned a last corner before pulling into Copenhagen's huge main train terminal.

"Copenhagen, Main Station!" announced the conductor.

The train made a final lurch and came to a stop with a hiss and a screeching of brakes. Mrs. Andersen held on to the back of her seat and frowned.

"It's too late, Mom." Peter looked out the window at the train platform. "There they go ahead of everybody. Eyebrows and Tattoo. Looks like they're in a hurry. "

They looked out the window at the figure of the little man hurrying through a crowd of people. The tall man with the tattoo limped along behind with old suitcases in both hands.

"Well," huffed Mrs. Andersen. "I don't suppose it would do any good to chase after him, but I'd sure like to give that character a piece of my mind. Imagine the nerve!"

Peter watched as the man disappeared around a corner. "At least we'll never see him again," he said as he picked up the small backpack he had stored under his seat. "But does that mean we can't go see the king, now that we don't have an invitation?"

"I'm sure they'll have our names," Mrs. Andersen reassured them. "We'll simply tell them who we are."

Peter tried to smile. "We just have to make sure that guy doesn't show up at the palace and tell the king *he's* Peter Andersen."

Elise didn't laugh at Peter's joke as she picked up her bag. "We need to call Dad so he can come meet us here at the station, don't we, Mom?"

An Unexpected Guest

"Okay," announced Mrs. Andersen. "Stay close together—I don't want to lose you in this crowd. And tell me if you see a telephone."

Or those two guys, thought Peter.

Their mother struggled with her large suitcase, setting it down every few yards. Peter's bags were heavy, too, and he didn't mind having a rest. Mrs. Andersen looked at her wristwatch.

"Four o'clock," she said, even though Peter and Elise could easily see the time on the large clock on the wall of the station, just below what looked like a mile-high ceiling. Peter smiled with amazement at the wonderful confusion of train whistles, train engines, and shouting people that filled the warm, smoke-filled air.

On the far side of the station, past an older man in a crowded little newsstand, Peter thought he saw the dark green booth of a public telephone.

"Mom, over there," he pointed, and they steered their caravan through the crowd of people to the phone.

"All right, you two stay together while I try to telephone your father," instructed Mrs. Andersen, searching her purse for the number her husband had given her. "Stay with the bags."

Peter and Elise both nodded as they arranged their pile of belongings outside the phone booth and sat down. Peter watched the crowd from their train make their way past.

"I wonder what happened to your circus performer," said Peter, looking from face to face for the people they had watched earlier on the train.

Elise stood up. "Well, at least the Polish scientist isn't around anymore."

"Yeah, that's sure a relief. He was really creepy."

"But look at this," said Elise, twirling around with her arms held out. "This is going to be great! We've never stayed at a hotel in the big city before."

"Never stayed in a hotel, period," answered Peter. "And don't forget we're going to go to your favorite amusement park in the world!"

"Tivoli!"

"I want to go on the roller coaster and the little boats on the lake." Peter imagined himself doing a loop on the ride.

"I can't wait to see the shows." Elise pretended to sing.

"The marching bands."

"The food."

"I'm trying to remember what it was like," Peter told his sister. "Do you remember?"

"No," answered Elise, practicing what looked like a ballet step. "We were only three last time we went, remember?"

"Yeah," replied Peter. They watched people rush to greet another trainload of arrivals. Some shook hands, others hugged, but everyone seemed to have someone waiting for them.

Except one little golden-haired girl crouching near a bench on the opposite side of the station. Not more than five or six years old, she looked out at the crowds with wild-eyed confusion, as if she was looking for a familiar face.

"Look over there, Peter." Elise pointed at the little girl.

"I see her," answered Peter. "But I don't see her mom."

By that time the little girl had put her head in her hands and started to cry.

Elise glanced around the train station with a worried look on her face. "Well, I don't know about you, but I think she's lost. I'm going to go talk to her."

Peter looked into the phone booth, but his mother was dialing once more, her back to them.

"Mom." Elise knocked on the door of the phone booth. Mrs. Andersen signaled for her to wait and tried to plug her other ear. Another train came into the station, which made everything vibrate. Mrs. Andersen started to shout.

"Yes, I'm looking for a Mr. Arne Andersen," Peter heard her say above the roar of the train. "ANDERSEN!"

Elise knocked once more, but their mother would only hold up her hand as she shouted something else into the phone. Peter looked over to where he had last seen the little girl, but the train had pulled in between them, blocking the view.

"We have to go see if she's okay, Peter," Elise finally announced. "You stay here with Mom and tell her where I went."

"I'm not letting you run around here by yourself," Peter protested.

"So come on. It's just right over there. We'll be right back."

"But Mom said—" Peter hesitated for a moment, then followed his sister around the platform and over to the bench where the little girl had been crying. The crowd from the train that had just pulled in was marching by.

"Where is she?" asked Peter, looking around a six-foot pile of luggage and trunks. "Wasn't she sitting right over here?"

They looked around the bench, then behind a baggage cart.

"Looks like she's gone," Peter decided. "Her mom must have found her."

They were about to go back to the phone booth when Peter thought he heard a sniffle, a short choke of a sob.

"What was that?" asked Elise.

"Yeah, I heard it, too," Peter added quietly. He looked around the back of the pile of luggage, then noticed that there was a small space in between two trunks. The little blond-haired girl was hiding inside what looked like a small fort made out of luggage.

"There she is." Elise's voice grew softer.

"Hey, come on out of there," Peter called into the fort. "Little girl . . ."

But the little girl glanced over her shoulder with a look of fright and tried to burrow backward, deeper into the pile.

"Don't do that, little girl," warned Peter. "It's all going to fall down right on top of you!"

But the girl either didn't hear or didn't care. As she pushed deeper under the pile of suitcases, several duffel bags on the top began to teeter.

"Watch out!" yelled Elise as the bags and several suitcases started to fall.

Peter tried to dive for the little girl, hoping at least to reach her before a trunk fell on top of her. He grabbed for a leg but missed just as the sharp corner of a large black suitcase caught him on the back of the leg.

"Ow!" Peter tried to pull back, but the suitcase pinned him down.

"Did you catch her?" Elise yelled from somewhere behind him. "Where did she go?"

"Out the other side!" replied Peter, pulling at his leg. "She got away, Elise!"

Finally Peter was able to crawl free and climb back out of the pile of suitcases. Elise was running after the little blond girl, toward the end of the platform. Peter stood up to follow when someone grabbed him by the collar from behind.

"What do you think you're doing playing in there?" came a man's gruff voice. Peter looked into the stern gaze of an older man with a long gray mustache, dressed in a uniform a lot like that of the train conductor. The man mopped his forehead with a handkerchief as he spoke. Peter guessed he was a porter, a luggage attendant.

"Uh . . . uh, I'm not playing, sir," squeaked Peter, pointing toward his sister. "We just saw this little girl crying over here. She was hiding under the suitcases, and then they fell."

"Oh, a little hide-and-seek, eh?" The porter still wasn't convinced, and he wasn't letting go of Peter's collar.

"No, sir, nothing like that. My sister is trying to catch her so we can find out what happened to her mom." Peter squirmed and tried to see where Elise had run to. "Honest, sir, we aren't playing, just trying to help this little girl."

Finally the man seemed to ease his grip, and he pushed his little round cap back on his head. "It's kids like you that get hurt, thinking this is some kind of playground. Off with you, now, and don't come back."

Finally the man let go of Peter's shirt, and Peter hurried away. Elise was near the end of the platform, still looking.

"Haven't you found her yet?" Peter asked as he hurried to join her.

"She's good at hiding," replied Elise. "Maybe she ran up into the train."

The train was still steaming beside them, and Peter wondered the same thing. But then he remembered something else.

"Mom's going to be looking for us," he told his sister. "Maybe we should go get her help."

Peter turned to go back around the train when he saw a flash of golden hair below them and off the side of the platform, some four feet down and next to the train track.

"It's her!" Peter whispered to Elise. They looked down off the edge of the platform to see the girl huddled under the edge, shivering and crying. She looked up to see them, pulled away from her hiding place, and ran down the track.

"Wait!" shouted Elise. "We're not going to hurt you!"

But Elise's yell was drowned out by the deafening whistle of yet another train. Peter looked up in horror to see the front end of a steam-belching locomotive sliding down the track on what looked like a collision course with the little blond girl!

Elise saw, too, and tried to shout even louder. An elderly couple from the train on the other side of the platform stopped to see what all the noise was about. And down on the track, the little girl froze in fear. She stood still, watching the approaching train, with nowhere to run. She only clutched what looked like a stuffed animal to her chest and put her head down while the train let out a deafening screech of its whistle.

She can't do that! Peter told himself as he jumped down to the track. He reached the little girl in three bounds, lifted her by the waist, and jumped to the side. He thought there would be just enough room to squeeze up next to the platform as the train rolled by.

"Peter!" yelled Mrs. Andersen from up above.

Peter didn't have time to answer. He just pressed the little girl against the sooty black concrete platform and tried to squeeze in beside her.

There has to be enough room, he told himself, face to the concrete.

But when the train didn't come, he looked up and over at the empty track.

Where did it go? he wondered. Then he saw the train pulling onto another track over on the other side of the station. No one else even seemed to notice.

"Peter!" yelled his mother. "What are you doing down there?"

Peter looked at the little girl and got to his feet. This time he wasn't going to let her get away. And she was so wide-eyed that it looked as if she had forgotten to cry.

"I'm fine, Mom," he answered back, as if he jumped in front of trains every day. After pulling Elise out from between the cars, and now this, Peter was beginning to think maybe the trains were after them.

"Come on," he told the filthy little girl, brushing off her worn, thin-looking sweater. Peter couldn't quite tell what color it had once been. She hugged an ancient, furless teddy bear but didn't say a word.

"Really, little girl." Peter helped her up to the platform, which was almost as tall as his shoulders. "This isn't a good place to hide."

"Peter!" repeated Mrs. Andersen once more after they had climbed back up. "I turn my back just two minutes, and now you're jumping down onto the train tracks. What is going on here?"

"We were just trying to help." Peter knew they had a good reason for doing what they did, but explaining it was a little harder. "This little girl was scared, so—"

"Elise told me all about that," interrupted Mrs. Andersen, pulling them away from the small crowd that had gathered on the platform to watch the commotion. Several porters had run over to see what was going on.

"She was lost," explained Peter to the gray-haired man who had scolded him earlier.

The man frowned and looked Peter over for a long moment, then he just twirled his mustache with his fingers and turned on his heel.

Mrs. Andersen, in the meantime, was shaking her head. "Peter, I thought we talked about this on the train, didn't we? You and Elise have to come back down to earth and stop this secret agent kind of stuff. Do you understand what I'm saying?"

Peter sighed and nodded. "We're not trying to do anything wrong, Mom, honest."

"Peter's right," agreed Elise. "We're not trying to get into trouble. It just seems to come to us."

At least the little girl didn't seem to want to run away anymore. Mrs. Andersen gently held the girl by the shoulders as she sat down next to her on a bench. But the girl wouldn't lift her head; she only stared at the ground. Her sweater was even more torn than Peter had first seen, probably thanks to Peter "saving" her from the train. And her homemade gray dress was even more dirty and threadbare. Her hair was a golden tangle that looked a lot like a bird's nest. Peter wondered if he looked as bad.

"Now, young lady," began Mrs. Andersen. "You're going to be fine. Can you tell us your name? Where's your mother?"

The girl said nothing, only stared at the ground and traced circles on the cement floor with her foot.

"It's all right," crooned Mrs. Andersen, gently lifting the girl's chin and looking into her face. "We're going to find your mom and dad. Do you understand what I'm saying? Did they come on the train with you?"

Still the girl said nothing. But Elise noticed something pinned to the front of the girl's dress, and she reached over to see what it was. The girl pulled back in fear and clutched her stuffed bear even more tightly than before. It was as grimy and torn as she was.

"Oh, I'm sorry," apologized Elise. "I was just going to see what this was. I didn't mean to scare you." But Elise slowly pulled back the girl's sweater to reveal a tattered name tag—or at least what was left of it. They all looked at the faded writing.

"Her name is Johanna," announced Elise. "Is your name Johanna?"

At the mention of her name, the girl's eyes seemed to brighten, and she looked up hopefully at Elise.

"Johanna," whispered the girl in a solemn little voice. Then she held up her bear for Elise to see.

Elise glanced at her mother, who was crouching by the bench. "She doesn't understand a word we're saying."

Mrs. Andersen nodded. "Yes, I see that now."

"Here, let me see," said Peter, taking the name tag. He read the little girl's first name, printed in large block letters in the middle of the torn piece of paper. Above the name was part of an address: *Lindenstrasse 67.* A German address.

"Did you come on the train?" asked Elise. But this time she spoke in German.

The little girl's eyes grew even wider, and she nodded.

"I'm sorry we scared you," Elise continued in a hushed tone, using the German she had learned in school. "We're your friends. Do you have a mother and father?"

"My father died," the girl whispered in German, almost too softly to understand. She looked at her furless bear when she said it, making the arms move as if the animal were speaking.

"What about your mother?" continued Elise. "Did she . . ."

"Mutter died, too. They made us take the train." She didn't take her eyes off the bear when she spoke, and she moved her animal like a puppet—as if he were talking and not her.

That's how it lost all its fur, thought Peter.

Elise bent over to see the little girl. "And then what?"

"Everyone else went away, too. When the planes came. The bombs."

Peter got the feeling that he was watching a puppet show, with the bear whispering and the little girl hiding behind her stuffed animal.

"Oh, I'm sorry," Elise got down on her knees in front of the little girl and took her hand. The girl nodded and looked down again.

"Mom, it sounds like she doesn't have any parents." Elise translated the rest of what the girl had said for her mother, who didn't understand very much German.

"She's an orphan, all right," announced Peter, reading the back of the girl's name tag. "Look, it says right here."

Mrs. Andersen nodded and straightened up. "I wish your father would hurry up and get here. He said he just had to finish up his meeting."

"How long is that supposed to be?" asked Elise, sounding worried.

"Maybe forty-five minutes. But that was before you two disappeared."

It turned out to be sooner than that—only fifteen minutes later. But the welcoming smile on Mr. Andersen's face turned to a question mark when he saw the little girl, who was still hiding shyly behind her stuffed bear.

"Who's this?" he asked Mrs. Andersen, scratching his sandy-colored hair. Peter thought his father always seemed extra tall and important looking in his black banker's suit and tie.

"The trip went fine," began Mrs. Andersen.

"Except for the spy," put in Peter.

"And now the kids seem to have found a little German orphan girl," finished their mother. "Somehow she must have been separated from her group."

Mr. Andersen shook his head in amazement and looked at Peter and Elise. "How long have I been away from you two, and all this has happened already? What is this spy business?"

"Not a spy," Mrs. Andersen assured him. "Just the runaway imaginations of two twelve-year-olds. The big question now is what do we do with little Johanna?"

Mr. Andersen nodded his head and looked down at the little girl. "I hear they've been sending them to relocation camps up here until they can find them homes again in Germany," he said as he squatted down to Johanna's level. He tried a few words of broken German, then gave up. "She probably doesn't speak Danish?"

"No," answered Mrs. Andersen. "But Elise is getting more good use out of her German."

"Well," said Mr. Andersen, standing up once more. "I'm glad we have an interpreter. Let's see what we can do about getting this little girl back to where she belongs."

But the train station manager was no help.

"I wish I could do something for you," he told them as he chewed an apple core down to the stem and seeds. He leaned back in his big leather office chair, and with his free hand the man fanned his face with a folded newspaper. His office smelled like cigar smoke.

"Hot lately," observed the station manager. "Hottest July I can remember for a long time."

"Yes, right," agreed Mr. Andersen, mopping his brow with a handkerchief. "But explain to me again about this little girl. Are you saying—"

"All I'm saying is we get lots of those groups through here, all the time. I have no authority in this kind of matter. You'll have to take it up with the police. Station is just down the road."

The police were just as friendly, but not much more helpful.

"The only thing I can do today is take her to a social welfare center," a middle-aged man told them from behind the tall oak counter. Peter had to stand on his tiptoes to see over the top. "And normally that's what we would do. Right now, though, that place is filled to the brim with refugees. We sent three families there last night, and they're all sleeping on the floor. Nobody has any room for these people right now."

"Mom," pleaded Elise. She was still holding Johanna's hand. "We can't just leave her. She's still scared to death. Can't we take care of her for a couple of days, until the police figure out where she really belongs?"

"Elise is right, Arne." Mrs. Andersen looked up at her husband. "At least until the police find a place for her."

"Now, if you're willing to give this little girl a place to stay for a while," said the policeman, taking a piece of paper from a desk drawer, "I'll just have you sign a little paper work. We can contact you in a week or two, when things settle down and we find a permanent place for her."

Elise tugged on her father's coat sleeve. "Please, Dad?" she asked.

Mr. Andersen looked down at the scared little girl, then sighed and nodded.

Secret in the Closet

"Wow!" said Peter in amazement, looking around at the ornate lobby of the hotel they had stepped into. The walls were paneled in rich walnut, and paintings of country scenes of wheat fields and windmills hung everywhere. Just like at the police station, their father stood talking with a clerk who stood behind a tall counter.

"Yeah, this is fancy, all right," agreed Elise, plopping down in a comfortable chair in front of a tiled fireplace. She leaned her head back and flopped out her right hand. Johanna still held on to the left. "Cooler than outside, too. The Hotel d'Angleterre!"

Peter looked over at his father, who was still leaning over the counter. The clerk, an older gentleman with wispy gray hair, knitted his eyebrows together and folded his hands as if he were praying.

"Maybe you could check the list again," insisted their father. "The arrangements were made through my bank. I know I was supposed to check in this morning, but my meeting was rescheduled, so I just couldn't make it until now. There has to be a room."

"I'm terribly sorry, sir." The clerk nervously washed his hands in the air, then mopped his damp forehead with a handkerchief. "There are just no rooms available. I don't know how this could have happened."

Peter slid out of his chair to see what was happening just as a middle-aged woman appeared behind the counter. She wore small, round spectacles, and her short, dark hair was cut precisely.

"Is there a problem, Knud-Ole?" asked the woman.

"Oh yes . . . I mean, no, Mrs. Petersen." The clerk looked relieved to see her, and repeated what he had just told Peter's father. From the way they talked, Peter gathered that the woman was the hotel manager. She shuffled through the pages of a book on the counter, then looked up at Mr. Andersen and back down at her book.

"Hmm." She turned some more pages. "Perhaps we can call around the city to find you another room. Unless you wouldn't mind staying in Room 14 or 15."

Mr. Andersen threw up his hands. "I should mind? What are they . . . haunted?"

The manager smiled slightly. "It's just that we haven't had a chance to . . . well, refurbish those two rooms since the Germans left. They still need to be cleaned, repainted, and such. However, we can make up the beds and place you there temporarily, as long as you understand . . ."

Mrs. Andersen pulled at her husband's arm. "That sounds fine, Arne. I'm not going to go out walking the streets again with all our suitcases and little Johanna."

"Yeah, Dad," echoed Elise, who had joined them at the counter. "That's fine. This is a neat place."

Mr. Andersen nodded his head as he signed the register. "Okay, we'll take the room with the German ghosts."

"Very good, then." Mrs. Petersen smiled at them. "I hope you'll have a pleasant stay. Knud-Ole will show you to your room."

She turned and disappeared into the back room once more.

The clerk turned back to the large board where he hung all the keys to the rooms, paused, and scratched his head.

"Is anything else wrong?" asked Mr. Andersen.

"The ghosts must have left with one of the keys," said the clerk softly. "I'm sure there were two keys here just a little while ago." He shrugged. "Well, I'll give you this one. Maybe the maid misplaced the other."

The clerk chuckled as he helped them down the hallway with their bags. "Room 14," he told them, as if it was some kind of secret. "That was the room the general stayed in."

"Really?" asked Peter. "A general?"

The clerk nodded. "General von Hanneken. And you would have thought that he'd be a little different. But they were all the same. They took over this hotel for more than three years—took everything that wasn't bolted down when they left. Ashtrays, towels, everything. I thought one or two of them would try to leave with their sheets and blankets."

Room 14 was up a short, open flight of stairs and down to the end of the hall.

"This is the general's room?" Peter asked as they walked in. The green velvet curtains were still hanging above the window, but two large beds were bare, and an easy chair was stacked upside down in the far corner.

"Here, let me get that chair," volunteered the clerk. "And we'll have a maid make up the beds immediately."

"And the extra cot?" asked Mr. Andersen.

"Right away."

Even without the sheets, the room looked to Peter like something out of a Hollywood movie. Wallpaper angels flew across the top edge of the walls. Highly ornate woodwork decorated the window and door. Peter stuck his head out the window and enjoyed the impressive view of Niels Juhls Street. A few cars and trucks shared the evening traffic with a sea of people on bicycles. And like an island in a rushing river, a large statue of one of the old kings of Denmark perched in a small park in the middle of the avenue.

"Who's that out there, Dad?" asked Peter. "The statue?"

"Christian the Fifth," answered their father, looking over Peter's shoulder. "Remember your history? He was the king who wrote up the old Danish law. . . ."

But Elise wasn't ready for a history lesson just yet. "Look," she told Johanna as they explored the room. "We even get our own washbasin and mirror." She held little Johanna up to see herself in the mirror, and tried the faucet while Johanna held her stuffed animal up to the mirror, too.

"*Bär?*" asked Peter, using his limited German. "Bear?" He could understand German almost as well as Elise but hadn't picked up the speaking part quite as well.

"*Ja,*" squeaked the little girl, making the bear bow low in front of Peter and offering him a paw. "*Mein name ist Alfred.*"

Peter smiled and shook the bear's paw, then looked up at Elise. "So her bear's name is Alfred, huh? I'll have to remember that. He seems like an important guy."

Elise and Johanna went on to look at the rest of the room while Peter explored the closet. Something was hanging in the far corner—a coat that smelled of mothballs and stale cigar smoke.

"Elise, look at this," he told them, pulling out the coat.

Elise looked more closely. "That must have belonged to the general."

It was a gray German officer's coat, stripped of medals or patches and frayed around the edges. Peter checked the pockets, but they were empty.

"Hey, did you know this uniform was in here?" asked Peter just as the hotel clerk came in with more suitcases. The man stopped short when he saw the coat and wrinkled his forehead.

"I can take that for you," he said, reaching out for the coat. He took it out of the room, holding it with two fingers as if it were full of fleas.

"Where did Mom go?" asked Elise, looking down the hall. Little Johanna looked with her, always a close shadow.

"She and Dad went to check about something to eat," replied Peter. "Wonder if there's anything else in the closet," Peter said to himself as he slipped inside the large walk-in room once more. The dust made him sneeze, and he felt along the wall for a light switch. *Maybe there's something more in the back*, he thought—just as the door slammed shut behind him.

"Hey, what's going on?" he yelled. "Elise!"

All he heard was a giggle on the other side of the door. "Elise, it's dark in here!"

More giggles.

"Elise, I'm going to get you!"

Peter felt his way along the floor, groping for the edge of the door in the dark. Something came loose in his hand—a piece of wood. *What's this?* The wood trim along the floor came away from the wall.

"Elise, I mean it," he said, pushing against the inside of the door. "I just broke something. You're going to get in trouble when Dad gets back. Open up right now."

"The door's open," replied Elise, and it gave way when Peter pushed it.

When he crawled out Elise was sitting on one of the beds, smiling.

"What were you doing in there?" she asked, holding her hand over her mouth.

"Nothing," replied Peter. "And you didn't scare me at all. But I think I broke something."

"No you didn't," answered Elise, kneeling down on the floor where Peter had pulled off the piece of floor trim. "There's a hole in here. Look."

"Must be a mousehole," said Peter, looking at the piece of wood.

Elise shook her head. "Not a mousehole, Peter. Look."

"Elise, don't put your hand in there. Whatever's in there might bite."

"Oh, it's all right." Elise reached into the hole and her arm disappeared up to the elbow. She gasped in pain, then yelped and fell over, her arm shaking violently. Johanna screamed.

"Elise!" Peter sprang over to help her, but she only smiled and stopped her act.

"Fooled you," she told Peter with a slight grin. "But there is something in here. Feels like . . ."

"You're getting worse all the time," Peter complained. "You never used to be like this."

"Sorry." Elise pulled out an old leather pouch, about the size of a pencil case.

"What's that?" asked Peter, taking the pouch. "Looks like one of those pipe tobacco pouches."

"Looks like it," agreed Elise. "Open it up."

But the zipper wouldn't budge. Peter's face turned red and he grunted. "This thing is really stuck," he finally admitted.

"Here, let me try."

Peter shook his head. "I've got it," he said, gritting his teeth.

"Come on," complained Elise. "You're going to break it."

Finally Peter threw it down on the floor. "There's something hard inside. But I'll bet you can't get it open either."

Elise picked up the pouch, yanked the stuck zipper a couple of times, and gently pulled it open.

"How did you do that?" asked Peter. Elise shrugged.

"Just have to leave it to a girl," she teased, peeking inside the heavy pouch. "But ooh, look here."

"Let me see. Let me see."

With a little bow Elise dumped a large black key out on the bed. "Ta-da!"

Peter caught his breath just as their parents came back in from the hallway.

"Look what we found in the closet, Dad," explained Peter. "And there was a German army coat in there, too, but the hotel clerk took it. Look."

Elise held the key up as everyone gathered around.

"That's a big one, all right," said Mr. Andersen. "A little rusty, is all. But big as your hand. It must open something major."

Elise wasn't so sure. "Why would someone hide a key in such a sneaky place?" she wondered.

Peter and Elise both looked at their father, but he only shrugged. "You're the detectives. Maybe a worker left it in there somehow. Why don't you ask at the front desk?"

Mrs. Andersen hit her husband playfully on the shoulder. "Now, don't you go giving them ideas, Arne."

Under the Door

Peter woke suddenly the next morning and sat up from his cot. Elise and Johanna were still asleep in their bed next to him, but his father was already up and shaving.

"Dad, you're up!" Peter exclaimed.

"Shh," whispered Mr. Andersen, his face full of foamy shaving cream. "Let them sleep."

Peter looked over at the little square folding travel clock his parents had propped up next to their bed. Seven o'clock.

"What time does Tivoli open?" Peter asked, slipping out of bed and standing next to his father.

Mr. Andersen chuckled and cut a trail with his razor through the shaving cream on his cheek. It smelled like pine trees or peppermint; Peter couldn't decide which. "Not for a few hours, Peter. You'll get there soon enough. It's going to be hot again today."

Elise sat up at the sound of their talking.

"Ready to go, Elise?" Peter teased. "Five minutes."

"Uh-huh." Elise stretched and looked over at where Johanna was stirring. "Mom said last night we're going to go out first thing and find Johanna some clothes to wear. Then we can start trying to find out where she belongs."

"Clothes," Peter groaned. "Doesn't she already have summer clothes?"

"Nothing she can wear!" Elise was clearly disgusted with her brother.

"Well, you heard the lady," said Mr. Andersen, dabbing his chin with a towel. "Clothes first, then Tivoli."

"But first something to eat," said Mrs. Andersen, waking up to the conversation as well. By then Johanna was awake, looking terrified again. She started to cry, but Elise put an arm around her and spoke softly in German.

"I'm sure glad that God brought you to us," Elise told the still-frightened little girl. "Did you know that you and Alfred are going to the amusement park with us today? And we're going to find you some nice new clothes, too. Won't that be fun?"

Little Johanna finally nodded and stopped sniffling. "Will there be any soldiers at the park?" she made her bear ask Elise. "*Soldaten?*"

"Nein. No, Johanna," promised Elise, looking right at the little girl. "All the mean soldiers have gone home. There are only nice people at Tivoli now."

"No soldiers? You're sure?" Alfred waved his arms.

"No soldiers," repeated Elise with a smile. She poked the teddy bear playfully in the nose.

Peter turned to the window and peeked out under the shade. Below there was a huge parade of bicycles—more than he had ever seen back home in Helsingor. Sidewalk-to-sidewalk bicycles, with an unfortunate truck or two stuck in the middle of the crowd. Everyone seemed to have someplace to go, and they were in a pleasant Wednesday morning workday kind of hurry.

"Looks like everybody in Copenhagen is going to work this morning," said Peter.

"Including me," said Mr. Andersen, adjusting his tie. "I have to be at a breakfast meeting in forty-five minutes. But you three—I mean, you four are going to have a great day. And I'm going to meet you at Tivoli after work. They're having fireworks tonight."

"We'll walk down with you to the restaurant for some break-fast," said Mrs. Andersen, coming out of the dressing room. By then the girls were dressed, too, and they all piled out of their room and out to the hallway. Peter felt his pocket for the big key they had found the night before.

"I have the key," he announced.

Elise looked at him. "Oh, you mean the key I found last night?"

"You mean the key *we* found," Peter corrected her. "I think I'd better keep it in my pocket for safety."

Elise just shrugged and held Johanna's hand. "Fine with me. I'm not going to lug it around with me. That thing is huge."

Mr. Andersen left them when they arrived at the lobby, and Mrs. Andersen was about to lead them to the hotel's small coffee shop when Peter remembered something.

"Mom, I forgot," he told her, backing up. "I left my pocket-knife in the room. Can I borrow the key to get back in?"

"They'll give you a knife in this restaurant," Elise told him with a straight face. "You don't have to bring your own."

"Thank you, Miss Manners," Peter answered her teasing with a smile. "But the last time I forgot my knife was when we got caught in that lifeboat and then got dragged out to the German submarine. I promised myself I'd never go anywhere without it after that."

Elise nodded. "I remember that. I suppose that old knife comes in handy sometimes."

"Can I, Mom?" Peter held out his hand. "I'll be right back."

Mrs. Andersen reluctantly gave Peter the room key but held on to it for a moment. "Meet us right back here. Do you remember how to get back to the room?"

"Sure, I think." Peter sprinted back down the hall with the key before his mother could change her mind, took the short flight of stairs in a leap, and slowed down.

"Wait a minute," he whispered to himself. "I think I went down the wrong hallway."

The rooms didn't quite look familiar, and Peter tried to remember the room number. It didn't occur to him to look at the key.

"Oh, here it is, I think." He was about to pull the key from his pocket when he thought he heard a shuffling sound from inside.

A maid? He hesitated. He stood outside the door for a moment, trying to decide what to do. Someone was definitely in the room.

My mirror! he thought, rummaging around in his pockets. He had forgotten his pocketknife, but at least he hadn't forgotten his mirror.

He pulled out the little mirror from his pocket and dropped quietly to the cool, polished wood floor—then quietly slipped the mirror under the small gap beneath the door. Fortunately, the door didn't close tightly against the floor, and as he tilted the mirror to get a better view, he caught sight of someone kneeling on the floor.

Doesn't look like a maid to me. He had been expecting a woman tucking in bed sheets. From the side, the man seemed vaguely familiar, but from under the door and backward through the mirror, Peter couldn't be sure. The man grumbled something, then plucked a cigarette from his mouth and threw it down on the floor.

Peter tried to adjust the mirror but couldn't see anything except the back of the man's head. One thing was sure, though: Whoever was inside was looking for something in the closet and rummaging around on the floor. Peter's heart beat faster when he realized what was going on.

The man grumbled some more, then turned toward the door. Peter almost dropped his mirror in surprise.

Mr. Eyebrows! What is he doing in our room?

He wanted to run, but Peter was so absorbed in what he was seeing that he didn't hear a cart rumbling down the hallway. It started to come around the corner before Peter realized what was going on. He jumped to his feet and stuffed the mirror into his pocket as a maid pulled into view.

"Good morning," the maid greeted him with a puzzled expression. "Are you lost?"

Peter shook his head no and started past her just as the door to their room burst open. But Peter didn't wait to see the man come out; he slipped around the same corner the maid had just come around and hurried to the stairway.

This would be the perfect time to slide down the railing, he told himself, flying downstairs. More than anything he wanted to disappear before the man caught up with him. He glanced quickly over his shoulder, but no one was there. Then to his left down in the lobby the ancient elevator rang, announcing the arrival of someone from another floor.

Peter reversed direction, stumbling backward up the wide staircase. From above he could see the top of a man's balding head as he stepped out of the elevator. The man hesitated, then turned down the hallway and away from the lobby.

Safe, breathed Peter, slipping back down the stairs. He tried to look casual at the bottom of the stairway, and glanced behind him as the figure of the man disappeared around a bend in the ground floor hallway. A door slammed somewhere out of sight, and when Peter peeked around the corner, the man was gone.

Hmm, thought Peter. *He's here somewhere. But where?*

He turned around and padded quietly back down the hall, through the empty lobby, and into the coffee shop. Elise and Johanna were just coming out of the double glass doors of the small restaurant that was connected to the hotel.

"Where have you been?" Elise asked him. "We've been looking all over for you!"

"Elise, you wouldn't believe who I just saw!" Peter told her, out of breath. "Eyebrows. The guy from the train!"

"No! Really?" She put her hands on her hips.

"Yes, really. And what's the German word for 'key'?"

"*Schlüssel*. Why?"

"Yeah, that's what he said." Peter reached down in his pocket to make sure he still had the big black key, then explained to his sister what he had seen.

"You'd better tell Mom," Elise told him as they returned to the restaurant. But their mother didn't give him a chance to explain.

"Oh, Peter, honestly." She looked exasperated when he began to tell her what he had done with the mirror. "You can't go looking under other people's doors. You really can't."

"But, Mom. It wasn't other people's rooms." Then he stopped to think for a moment. "Well, at least, I don't think so."

"Peter . . ." Mrs. Andersen put a hand to her forehead. "Do you mean to tell me that you were spying on someone, and you're not even sure which room it was?"

"Well, the hallways were a little confusing. But I'm pretty sure it was our room. Mom, he was looking for the key. I know he was."

Mrs. Andersen wrinkled her forehead and frowned. Then Peter thought of something.

"Look, I can prove it. We just have to go back and I'll show you. The man threw a cigarette down on the floor."

Elise wrinkled her nose. "Yech. In our room?"

"All right," agreed Mrs. Andersen with a sigh. She dabbed the corner of her mouth with a cloth napkin and stood up. "Let's go see what you're talking about. Maybe we can put this thing to rest."

"Great, Mom!" Peter took another breakfast roll and stashed it in his pocket for future reference as he followed her out of the little restaurant.

"So if this guy really was in the room," said Elise as they hurried down the hall, "it would smell like smoke, right?"

"No." Peter shook his head. "I don't think his cigarette was lit. But I saw him throw it down on the floor. I'll bet he was mad because he couldn't find the key."

"All right, Peter," said their mother as she carefully unlocked their room. A maid was just coming out of the room next door, broom in hand. "We're not going to meet a burglar here now, are we?"

"He's gone, Mom. But he was here. I just know he was."

Peter slipped into the room past his mother.

"I don't see anything," said Elise, looking disappointed.

Mrs. Andersen stood in front of the open door just inside the room and crossed her arms while Peter got down on his knees on the floor.

"He was right over here, Mom, honest." Peter got to his feet and acted out what he had seen. "Kind of in front of the closet. Then he stood up and threw it down, like this."

They all looked down at the floor at the place where Peter pointed.

"But I don't understand . . ." His voice tapered off. "I was sure that it was right here. Maybe he picked it up."

"I thought you said he came right out of the room and chased you," said Mrs. Andersen.

"Not exactly." Peter scanned the floor once more.

"I don't even see any ashes or anything," said Elise. Johanna was searching next to her, looking puzzled.

"Now, Peter," began Mrs. Andersen. "I'm sure you saw someone, but I really don't think it was in this room."

"Maybe it was the maid, Mom. Yeah. The maid already came and cleaned it up or something."

Mrs. Andersen held up her hand. "Okay, Peter, but they would have been pretty quick to have done that already. And honestly, you should hear yourself. A rude man on the train shows up here, of all places in this big city, the same hotel we're in, and now he's searching our room? Doesn't that sound a little farfetched, even to you?"

"But, Mom," Peter tried one more time.

"No more 'But, Moms.' We're going to enjoy the rest of our vacation without any more nonsense about a strange man in our room. Okay?"

Peter sighed. Maybe he wasn't so sure which door he had been looking under. "I guess so."

"That's better." Mrs. Andersen reached over to pat Johanna on the head. "I think finding little Johanna has been adventure enough. She doesn't need any more excitement."

Peter tried to imagine for a moment what the little girl had been through. He had seen pictures of German cities leveled by bombs, and thousands of people wandering the streets of Germany, looking for a place to stay. Johanna had probably come from one of those places. She had already seen too much for her young years. And how old was she, really? Five? Six? Peter shivered at the thought and felt a little guilty.

"But it really seemed like the same man we saw on the train," he added, his voice almost a whisper. "And I think I heard him say something about a key. 'Schlüssel.' That *is* the German word for key, right?"

Johanna looked up when she heard a word she recognized. "Schlüssel?" she asked.

Elise smiled at her. "That's it, Peter. But are you sure that's what he said?"

"Well, not totally. I couldn't really hear him. But I'm pretty sure." He paused and looked at his mother, who was putting a few things in her purse. "Kind of sure."

"Well, if you kids would rather stay here looking for burglars, that's okay with me." She straightened her hair in the mirror. "But I think I'm going to Tivoli."

Peter brightened up and grabbed his pocketknife from the bedside table. "No kidding?" he asked.

Mrs. Andersen smiled. "I promise we won't go shopping all day. Come on, let's get our things and go. Oh, and I have to check at the front desk for messages."

The man with the mustache, Knud-Ole, was on duty behind the front desk again that morning. Peter hung back after his mother continued on her way out the front door.

"Yes?" Knud-Ole looked curiously down his nose at Peter.

"Um, I was just wondering." Peter took a quick look at the front entry. Elise was disappearing with Johanna.

It won't hurt to find out.

"I was just wondering if you have any Polish scientists who checked in about the same time we did. Maybe a little before."

The man studied Peter for a minute. "Polish scientists? I don't think I've heard that joke before. . . ."

"No joke," insisted Peter. "It's really a question. But I don't know his name. I just know he's supposed to be some kind of Polish scientist. At least, that's what he said."

"Oh, I see." The clerk nodded, smiled, and pulled out the hotel register from beneath the counter. "You're an investigator, and you want me to check for you, is that it?"

"Could you? I mean, I don't know if you can. But there were these two guys . . ."

"Maybe you could describe them to me?"

"Right." Peter looked over his shoulder again. Elise was coming back into the lobby, looking around. "Yeah, there was this short guy, kind of bald, except he has really bushy eyebrows. The other guy is taller and really muscly." Peter put his arms out like a gorilla's. "And he had this tattoo on his arm, kind of down by his wrist."

The man shook his head and clicked his tongue. "Sounds like a rough couple of fellows to me. Polish, you say?"

"Well, I don't know. That's what they said. But I suppose he could have been anything, really. German, Swiss, Austrian, maybe. I'm not sure."

"I see." The clerk looked up and down his list and shook his head. "Well, I'm not seeing anyone here like that. No, wait a minute. Here's a fellow. A Mr. Brezinski from Warsaw. Says he's here on business. Yes, and I suppose his eyebrows were a little, well . . . he checked into Room . . ."

Peter leaned forward. "Which room?"

"No, that's not right. That's the same room you're checked into. It's crossed out here on the register."

"What?"

Elise joined Peter and started pulling his elbow.

"Oh yes, now I remember what it was." The clerk pulled off his glasses, breathed on one of the lenses, and started polishing it with a handkerchief. "What is it about that room? That was the gentleman who specifically requested your room for some reason, but since there was still another clean room available at the time, we had to place him in that one. He started to insist, but then he changed his mind and said it was all right. Yes, I remember that now."

Peter nodded. "So which room is he in now?"

"Let's see." The man ran his finger down the page once more. "Twenty-two. Room 22."

"Thanks!" said Peter, backing away. "Thanks a lot."

The clerk gave him another curious look. Peter started to fall backward over a chair, but Elise caught him.

"Oh, and one other thing," said Peter, backing away toward the door and digging the big black key out of his pocket. "We found this key in our room, and we were wondering if it belonged to anyone."

Knud-Ole squinted at the key Peter held up, then frowned and shook his head. "That's a different kind of key. Maybe it belonged to one of our German . . . ah, guests. Go ahead and keep it. Souvenir."

"Right," answered Peter, flashing a grin. "Thanks!"

But the grin froze on his face when he looked across the lobby and noticed a familiar-looking man sitting in a low chair, staring at him over the top of a newspaper. The man quickly ducked behind his paper when Peter turned.

It's him . . . Mr. Eyebrows! He saw the key!

Peter panicked, backing out the front door. He only saw the man's telltale eyebrows, but that was all he needed to see.

"Hey, wait for me!" Peter yelled and ran as fast as he could.

TIVOLI ADVENTURE

"Everyone knows that the best view of the city is from the top of Our Savior's Church," Elise told them from several steps ahead. "And besides, there's probably a breeze up there, so we can cool off."

Peter had endured the stops at three department stores, and finally everyone was dressed and ready to go. Now Johanna looked like every other little Danish girl. And she seemed happy enough, as long as Elise held her hand. She even said a few words once in a while, with shy little smiles or giggles.

"I thought we were going straight to Tivoli after all this shopping business," replied Peter. "It's been all day. And it's too hot to be shopping."

"It's only been an hour," their mother assured them, looking at a bus schedule. "But you're right. It is getting warmer, even in the shade of the tall buildings here."

A crowd of bike-riding office workers breezed by them on the street, and Peter stood staring at the big statue of the city's founder, Bishop Absalon, on horseback. It was so realistic that the horse looked ready to hop off the big pedestal and gallop down the street.

"Good day for a horse ride," commented Peter.

Elise looked up and down the street. "Good day for shopping."

"No fair. Three girls against one boy."

"That's the breaks," answered Elise with a smile.

"Okay, first we're going to see the city," announced their mother. "And Elise is right. We'll just walk down this way to the Christiansborg Palace, where the Supreme Court and all the government people are, then over the Knippels Bridge, and then we're going to climb up to the top of Our Savior's Church for the breeze and the view."

"Then can we go to Tivoli?" asked Peter.

"Patience." Mrs. Andersen folded her map and started off down the sidewalk. After a few blocks, Peter had a chance to look around—and up. "One, two, three . . ." He counted stories on a vine-covered brick apartment building as they waited at a corner for a light to change. "Five, six, seven stories. Wow, these places are a lot taller than back home."

Without checking for traffic, Peter started to step back into the street to see better.

"Watch it, kid!" yelled a man on a bicycle, sweeping by Peter so closely that Peter felt the wind against the back of his neck.

Elise grabbed his wrist and pulled Peter out of the street.

"You're going to get run over, Peter," she scolded him. Peter looked around and shook his head.

"They drive like maniacs in this city," he observed.

"Peter, you're going to have to be more careful," his mother told him sternly. "This is Copenhagen, remember. Now, come on, you kids. We have a ways to go."

It wasn't long before they arrived at the Knippels Bridge across one of Copenhagen's harbor canals. Each end featured a tall tower, and countless rows of people on their black bicycles seemed to fly across. Below, on the inky-smooth water, a man in a small fishing boat was looking for a place to tie up between a coastal tugboat and another fishing cutter.

Just over the bridge they could see the towering, twirled shape of Our Savior's Church steeple. And ten minutes later they were high above the city on a balcony halfway up the tower. Below them, the city spread out for miles in a red-tile-roofed tapestry decorated with miniature streets.

"Ah, this is nice," sighed Peter. "You were right, Elise. There is a nice, cool breeze up here."

Even Johanna stared in wonder at the sight when Mrs. Andersen lifted her up so she could see over the railing.

"Does this look like home?" Elise asked Johanna.

The little girl shook her head. "Nein. No airplanes."

Elise smiled. "Well, this is bigger than any city I've ever seen. Makes Helsingor look like a little village. And it does feel a little cooler."

Mrs. Andersen pointed out the green copper towers that pointed like sharp fingers above all the roofs. "There's the Nikolaj Church, and the spiral one just over the bridge is the Stock Exchange."

Peter shaded his eyes and tried to see what his mother was pointing out. "And let's see, which direction is Tivoli from here?"

A man who was standing next to them lowered his binoculars. He looked older, almost their grandfather's age.

"If you're planning on going to Tivoli today, you'd best go early," he volunteered.

"Early?" asked Mrs. Andersen, putting little Johanna back down. The man nodded knowingly.

"It's going to be crowded tonight. The warm weather. Fireworks. And some kind of official parade is going by that way with the American General Eisenhower."

Elise clapped her hands. "General Eisenhower is going to be here, too?"

The silver-haired man smiled. "I can tell you don't read the papers very much, young lady."

No, she's just in them all the time, Peter thought with a smile.

"Schlüssel," whispered Johanna, turning back and tugging on the tall, old wooden door that opened out to the balcony.

"Here, Johanna, don't pull on that door," warned Elise.

But Johanna only put her finger in the large, rusty keyhole and looked back at Peter. "Schlüssel?" she repeated, her face looking like a question mark.

Elise stepped over and took Johanna's hand. "Remember 'schlüssel,' Peter? Key? She wants you to try our key in this big old lock here."

Peter shrugged. "Sure. Why not?"

He pulled the black key out of his pocket and carefully pushed it into the lock.

"Hey," he told them. "It fits."

But as hard as he tried, the key wouldn't turn. "At least, it almost fits."

The old man with the binoculars watched them curiously. "That's an old key you have there," he told them. "Probably fits something big."

———————

Tivoli was another half-hour walk across the city, but this time Peter led the way. "We should take the bus," he called back over his shoulder as yet another trolley clanged by them on rails set into the middle of the street. Sparks flew overhead where the trolley's arm reached up for power.

"Would you rather we spend our money on a trolley or on having a little fun in Tivoli?" asked Mrs. Andersen. Peter smiled and didn't answer. He just skipped ahead and looked for the big stone arch at the entrance to Tivoli Park.

"Or maybe you'd rather go around to all the oldest buildings in the city and try our key?" asked Elise.

"That's not such a bad idea," Peter called back as they rounded a corner. "It has to fit somewhere. But first, Tivoli."

But Elise groaned as she saw the entrance to the park. "Mom, look at all the people. That man at the church was right."

Peter stopped, too, and stared. "Are they all waiting for General Eisenhower, do you think?"

"Well, everybody loves a war hero," answered Mrs. Andersen. "Especially an American general like Eisenhower."

"Eisenhower?" It was the first time Johanna had said anything since they left the church tower. "What's Eisenhower?"

Elise smiled and crouched down. "Sounds like a German word, doesn't it? No, Eisenhower is the American general who helped stop the war, Johanna. He came from America to visit us."

Johanna nodded as if she understood. But by then they were elbow to elbow in the crowd in front of Tivoli's tall stone archway entrance.

"Step back!" ordered a policeman, hurrying along the street. Already, someone had stretched a rope along the edge of the sidewalk to keep people back.

"Stay together," said Mrs. Andersen, reaching for Elise's hand. Peter stood on his tiptoes to see over his sister's shoulder just as a long black convertible drew slowly by on the street in front of Tivoli. Someone started clapping, and soon everyone was cheering.

"Is that him?" Peter yelled into his sister's ear. There were two men in uniform sitting in the backseat, one of them an older Danish man whose picture Peter thought he had seen in the newspaper. Next to him sat a smiling General Eisenhower, waving to the crowds. A moment later, they were gone.

"That was it?" asked Elise, sounding disappointed.

"Well, that wasn't what we came to see, was it?" asked their mother. "That was just a little bonus."

Peter looked around at the crowd. A lot of people were going back into buildings; others were making their way into Tivoli Park. Across the street, two men stood with their arms crossed, staring straight at Peter and Elise. Peter caught sight of the bushy eyebrows.

"Elise, look over there," whispered Peter. She turned around to look in the direction Peter was pointing with his nose.

"Don't look so obvious," said Peter, "but I think I see Eyebrows and Tattoo on the other side of the street."

"What are they doing here?" whispered Elise.

Peter ducked behind a woman with a baby carriage. The woman pushing it looked at them suspiciously.

"Eyebrows saw us in the hotel lobby with the key," Peter told his sister. "He must have followed us."

Elise peered out from around the carriage.

"They're gone," she reported.

"Good thing," replied the young woman, pushing her baby carriage down the sidewalk.

Peter and Elise looked around for their mother, who had walked on ahead through the crowd. Peter stopped to tie his shoe.

"Hey, Mom, wait!" cried Elise, taking Johanna's hand. They started to trot through the crowd toward the park entrance. Peter felt for the big key in his left pocket, then looked for the way his mother had taken.

Before he could catch up, someone knocked into him from behind—hard. Peter felt a sharp blow on his back, almost as if someone meant to push him over on his face. But there was something else, too—almost too quick to notice. For a second it felt as if someone else's hand was in his pocket.

"Hey!" yelled Peter, falling face first to the sidewalk. He was able to put out his hand just in time, then got to his knees and looked around. All he could see was a group of preschool kids with their teachers in tow.

"Well, at least the key is still there," he said to himself, patting his pocket once more as he stood up. Whoever had pushed him was gone, and Peter couldn't even see where the person had disappeared to. He shivered for a moment, even in the heat. "They must really want that thing."

———

"Peter, I thought you were supposed to be enjoying yourself." Mrs. Andersen looked at Peter with a worried expression as he got off the roller coaster. "You look more like you're in pain."

"Oh no, Mom," said Peter, looking around the park. "I'm fine."

He didn't see the two men anymore and relaxed a bit. *I just feel bad my best friend isn't here*, he thought.

"This is great," Peter finally told his mother. "Johanna loves it."

"I can see Johanna is having the time of her life. But you, I'm not so sure."

Elise looked sideways at her brother as they strolled to the Chinese theater stage where clowns and mimes performed. "Lighten up," she told him. "Look at this place. Don't you wish our apartment building looked like the Chinese pavilion, with the curvy roof?"

Peter smiled but didn't laugh.

"And all the smells!" Elise closed her eyes and breathed in deeply, obviously trying to cheer up her brother. "I can smell sausages and flowers and a hundred other things. . . . Can't you?"

"I think so." Peter didn't close his eyes, but the thought of eating a Danish hot dog sounded pretty good just then. The kind served from an outdoor stand on a little paper plate without the bun, with a dash of spicy mustard. "I wish Dad could be here, instead of having to go to all those meetings."

"Well, Dad's going to meet us for dinner and then the fireworks, remember?"

"I know." Peter frowned.

"How about the music?" she tried once again. "Have you ever heard so much music? There's someone singing, there's an organ. . . . It sounds like a three-ring circus."

"Elise, he almost got the key right out of my pocket."

Elise stopped and frowned. "Okay, I can't cheer you up. So what was this about the key again?"

"Well, I'm sure it was one of those guys, since they followed us all the way from the hotel. I'm telling you, they tried to grab the key right out of my pocket!"

"Those that whisper tell lies," said their mother with a smile, leaning over to where the twins were talking. She liked to quote her favorite old Danish folk saying.

Peter swallowed hard. His mother always seemed to hear what they were saying. "Were we whispering?"

"Sounded like it to me, Peter. I hope you're not playing detective again."

"Mom, I saw them," said Peter. "And Elise saw them too this time. They were across the street from us, and they were watching us."

Mrs. Andersen sighed. "Who are we talking about now, or do I need to ask?"

"It's just creepy, Mom," answered Peter. "We keep seeing these two guys from the train, no matter where we go. They're following—"

Mrs. Andersen frowned and looked down at Johanna. "All right. I think your imagination is running a little wild here. I hope you're not worrying little Johanna about all this."

At the mention of her name, Johanna smiled up at Mrs. Andersen. Then she looked in wild-eyed amazement at a balloon seller. He was holding the strings of what must have been at least fifty rainbow-colored balloons, enough to float a small dog.

"Balloon?" she asked.

Peter and Elise both had to laugh at the little girl's expression. "Can we get her one, Mom?" asked Elise.

Mrs. Andersen smiled and reached into her purse for a coin. "With the money we saved by not taking the trolley."

Johanna clapped her hands with delight at the red balloon she chose, then tied the string around her teddy bear's hand. Peter gave up trying to explain to his mother what he had seen and tried to forget about the pickpocket.

They laughed at the clowns with the big shoes on the pantomime stage. They all got a chance to ride the boats in the pretty little Tivoli lake. Mrs. Andersen even gave Peter a coin to try his luck at knocking down a set of milk bottles at one of the carnival booths. He missed all three times.

"That's okay," Elise reassured him. Peter smiled back weakly.

Something else kept bothering him, though. He wasn't even sure what it was until someone looked sternly at Johanna after Elise asked her a question in German.

"Elise, they're looking at you," Peter whispered to his sister.

"I don't care," Elise replied back in her regular voice. "We're not saying anything wrong."

"But you're talking in German."

Elise shrugged. "You try talking in Danish to her. See how much she understands."

"That's not what I mean," he replied. "Maybe you could talk a little softer, then not so many people will hear you."

"I'm not going to whisper for the rest of the day," insisted Elise.

Peter sighed. He knew his sister was right, but he still couldn't help feeling embarrassed when people noticed.

"That was fun," said Johanna, smiling. "Did you like it, Peter?"

Peter looked around to see if anyone was watching before he nodded.

"Sure, Johanna," he told her in German. He could say that much. "Fun. Tivoli is a great place." He looked around one more time.

"They're not here, Peter," Elise reminded him quietly.

"Let's go on the roller coaster again," he suggested as they lined up one more time to go on a ride called the "Mountain Roller Coaster."

Johanna squealed with delight and Mrs. Andersen laughed.

"Look at her," she declared. "She's ready to go with you two kids anywhere. Here, I'll hold the balloon if you want to go again."

"Okay, one more time," Elise agreed, taking Johanna's hand.

They held on for yet another ride, flying up and down the rickety wooden hills and turns of Tivoli's biggest attraction. The best part was the top of the hill, when Peter could see out over the park in the middle of the huge city. But then the car flew down the steep track once more, bringing screams from the younger kids in the front car.

"That's it," gasped Elise after the ride, making her legs sway like limp macaroni. "I've had enough."

"Yeah, that's it," agreed Peter. His stomach still felt as if he had left it on the last turn. "No more."

He felt in his right pocket for the big key, then in his left. Both pockets were empty.

"Oh no," he moaned.

"What?" asked Elise.

"One more time?" asked Johanna.

"No way, Johanna," answered Elise. "What are you moaning about, Peter?"

Peter was down on his knees in the thick, waist-high bushes next to where the roller coaster loaded. "I lost the key."

A couple with their toddler stopped to stare curiously at Peter, but he didn't look up.

"The key! I lost the key!"

Elise stepped over to where Peter was searching. "Are you sure? We didn't turn upside down or anything."

"I know. But it's just gone." He shook one of the bushes and looked underneath. "Elise, it could be anywhere."

Elise looked with Peter for a few minutes but finally threw down her hands. "It's no use, Peter. It could be anywhere. In one of the roller coaster cars, in the tunnel. Anywhere."

"Yeah, I know," admitted Peter. "But if we don't find it . . ."

"Then what? We don't know what it fits anyway. And this isn't the first time you've lost something out of your pocket."

Peter stomped his foot and felt his ears get hot. "I don't care. We still have to find it."

Mrs. Andersen gave them a curious look as she returned from

the drinking fountain. "What are you kids doing over there in the bushes?" she asked as she gave Johanna back her balloon.

Elise shrugged. "Peter says he lost the key."

"The key? Oh, you mean that old rusty thing you found in the hotel?"

Peter pointed up at the tracks of the roller coaster. "I'm pretty sure it fell out while we were on this ride, Mom."

For the next ten minutes they searched the area around the roller coaster, walking slowly around a small fence. Above them they could hear the happy screams of others who were enjoying the ride. But Peter could only shove his hands in his pockets and grit his teeth in frustration as he kicked the bushes.

"I hate losing things like this," he said to himself. "I hate it. I hate it. I hate it."

"Peter." Elise pointed to the walkway with her eyes. Peter looked up long enough to see Eyebrows and Tattoo strolling through the park toward them as if they were out enjoying themselves like the rest of the crowd. Peter closed his eyes and held his breath.

Not again. Not one more time. Not now. Where's Mom?

"Peter," piped up Johanna from behind him. "Look! See what I found? Is this the key from the hotel?"

Peter was afraid to open his eyes, but he turned around to see Johanna standing proudly with the big black key in her hand, waving it high in the air for everyone to see.

Peter stepped quickly over to Johanna and retrieved the key.

"That's great, Johanna," he told her under his breath. "You found it."

Johanna looked pleased with herself and beamed at the others. "Are you glad, Peter?" she said in a loud German voice. "You found it once. Now I find it, too!"

"Shh." Peter patted the little girl on the shoulder.

But Johanna didn't understand. "Why 'shh,' Peter? I found it!"

Elise stepped over to them, glancing quickly at the two men. Tattoo had taken a good look at Johanna when she was holding up the key and was whispering something to his partner.

"You're really good at finding things, Johanna," Elise said sweetly. "I'm sure Peter is really glad that you found it. *Gut*, Johanna. Very good."

Finally Eyebrows and Tattoo made their move toward the twins and Johanna. Peter looked for a way to run, but the men split up and came at them from both directions.

"Hey, kids," said Eyebrows, again the spokesman.

Peter glanced around one more time for his mother. Elise gave Peter a worried look. *Where did Mom go?* he thought frantically.

"Small world, is it not?" Eyebrows forced a smile. Peter put his hand on his pocket and kept silent.

"We see you on the train," continued Eyebrows in his heavy accent. "And now here in Tivoli Park again. What a coincidence."

Peter nodded nervously, knowing it was no coincidence. Behind them, blocking the way, Tattoo stood like a guard.

"Listen, kids," said Eyebrows, giving up on the small talk. "You have something that doesn't belong to you. We know where it came from, and I'm going to return it so you don't get in trouble for stealing."

"Stealing?" Peter stalled.

"You know what I'm talking about. The old key. It belongs to someone else, and it's my job to return it."

"We haven't done anything wrong," said Elise, standing up straight.

"Of course you haven't," continued the man, smiling nervously and shifting from foot to foot.

"It's not yours!" Peter raised his voice and backed right into Tattoo, accidentally stepping on the man's foot.

"Ow!" complained Tattoo. He reached down to grab Peter by the shoulders, then let go as if he had touched hot coals.

"*Die Mutter*," grunted Tattoo. "It's the mother."

Eyebrows glanced quickly back over his shoulder at Mrs. Andersen, who was making her way through the crowds to where they were standing. He hesitated only a second, frowned at Peter, and then grabbed Tattoo by the arm.

"Forget it," he muttered to his partner in German. "I have another idea."

Peter and Elise could only wait helplessly for their mother to arrive while the two men disappeared into the crowd in the other direction. "Mom!" Peter cried as soon as his mother was close enough to hear. "It was those guys again."

"What?" Mrs. Andersen looked puzzled.

"Those guys from the train!" Elise chimed in. She and Peter took turns explaining what had happened, while their mother looked from the twins to Johanna, who didn't quite know what was going on.

"All right," she finally told them with a serious expression. "I'm sure there's some explanation for this. I'll have your father talk to them when we get back to the hotel."

————

"So how did you enjoy the fireworks, Master Peter?" asked the clerk, Knud-Ole, from behind the main desk as they all dragged into the hotel late that night.

Peter couldn't help yawning, but he managed to grin.

"The fireworks were great," he replied, clapping his hands together over his head. "Boom! Like shooting stars. And all different colors, too."

Elise nodded her head in agreement. "The whole city must have been there. They were terrific."

Mrs. Andersen put her hand on Peter's and Elise's shoulders and guided them through the lobby, while Mr. Andersen carried Johanna in his arms.

"They were terrific, all right," said Mr. Andersen quietly. "But I know three tired children who are going to get right to bed. It's way past your bedtimes. And tomorrow we're supposed to meet the King of Denmark."

Peter smiled and yawned once more as he tripped over the Turkish rug in the empty lobby. He dragged one foot after another down the hallway and up the short flight of stairs, holding on to his sister to tow him up.

"Peter, you're too heavy," she told him.

"That's okay," he told her. "You're strong."

"Walk, Peter." But Elise continued to tow him up the stairs. "Tomorrow we—"

"Tomorrow we meet the king."

HIDE-AND-SEEK

"Peter, can you be quiet over there?" mumbled Elise. "You've been thrashing around for hours."

"Sorry," replied Peter from his cot. He tried not to move for a few minutes, until Elise's breathing over on the bed started to even out. A streetcar outside rumbled by, the wheels making a grinding *clackety-clack* as it passed by their window in the early morning. He could almost feel the rumble from below.

Inside the room, his father snored. His mother snored. Even Johanna was making a lot of noise.

She sleeps through everything, thought Peter. *Why doesn't Elise complain about the snoring?*

Finally Peter sat up and tried to peek out through the lacy curtains on their window. Out in front of the hotel, King Christian the Fifth still sat on his horse in the middle of the little park. The pale yellow glow from a streetlight seemed to make the statue glow.

What am I going to say to the king? Peter asked himself. But there were too many thoughts flying around inside his head. The key. The two men on the train. Losing the key. Seeing the American general. Eyebrows and Tattoo again, following them. Johanna finding the key right when they walked by. What was the key for, anyway?

His mind wandered, and he imagined himself tripping in front of the king, or forgetting his own name, or doing something stupid. So he sat for a while longer, worrying.

Peter finally fell asleep at the window, only to wake a short time later. He lay down once more as the morning light outside began to brighten the rooftops, then fell asleep again just as his dad's alarm clock went off.

"Up, up," announced Mr. Andersen, turning off the alarm. "This is the day the Andersen family meets King Christian!"

Peter tried to plug his ears and bury his face in his pillow, but Elise only shook him loose. "Come on, Peter sleepyhead. Today's the day."

"I'm not going," he groaned.

Elise only laughed.

"I'm not kidding, Elise. I don't feel very good. You guys go see the king, and I'll just stay here."

"If I go, you go," his sister replied. "Besides, I thought you were excited."

"I'm really tired." Peter felt the butterflies in his stomach. "Didn't sleep very good last night."

"Me neither," Elise replied. "I was just thinking all night. I think I was dreaming about it."

"You too? Did you figure out what we should do next?"

Elise shook her head. "Uh-uh. Maybe we'll have to take her home to Helsingor if we can't find her family."

Peter thought for a second about what his sister had just said. "Oh. I was thinking about the key, not Johanna."

"The key?" Elise's face fell. "Your silly key. It doesn't fit anything."

"It does, too. Otherwise, why would those guys be after it?"

"Well, Mom said Dad would go talk to them, didn't she? And

if you're so worried about it, why don't you hide it somewhere they can't find it?"

"Hmm," thought Peter, scratching his head. "That's not such a bad idea, Elise. But where should we hide it?"

Elise looked around. "Not anywhere in here."

Johanna sat up next to Elise, acting as if she understood what the twins were saying in Danish.

"Johanna, where should we hide the key?" asked Elise, half joking.

"The key I found yesterday?" Johanna didn't hesitate but held up her worn bear. She hadn't let go of the poor stuffed animal since they had first seen her in the train station. "Alfred can eat the key."

Peter smiled. "Right. Did she say eat?"

Then he thought for a moment, and it dawned on him. "Hey, can I see Alfred for just a second?"

Peter took the animal, turned it around, and found what he was looking for. One of the seams along the bear's waist was pulling apart, showing a gray cotton stuffing.

"Perfect." Peter reached over into his shoe on the floor, pulled out the big key, and poked it into the bear's stuffing. "All we have to do is sew it up a little. No one will ever find it in a little girl's stuffed bear, right?"

Their mother came back into the room. "Are you kids still here in bed? I thought you'd be dressed by now."

"We're getting up, Mom," Elise assured her mother.

"Well, I'm going with your father to a breakfast reception at a restaurant a couple of blocks away. The Grand Café. So we need you all to stay here in the hotel for just a couple of hours."

Elise smiled up at her mother. "We'll be fine."

"Are you sure you feel comfortable taking care of little Johanna by yourselves?"

"No problem, Mom," answered Peter. "We're going to be thirteen pretty soon, remember? Oh, but Dad, do you have time to go talk to those two guys? Mom said . . ."

Mr. Andersen looked at his wife for a moment, then down at his watch.

"The two men I told you about," Mrs. Andersen reminded him. "The kids said they were asking about the key. Something about it belonging to someone else. I told them you'd take care of it. Apparently the men, or one of them anyway, is staying here in the hotel."

Mr. Andersen sighed, then nodded. "All right. But only for a minute. Do we know which room they're staying in?"

"Twenty-two," answered Peter.

"Then you come with me and we'll clear this thing up."

Mr. Andersen led the way down the hall and up to the second floor, Peter galloping along behind. In a minute Mr. Andersen was rapping on the door of Room 22, ignoring the "Do Not Disturb" sign hanging from the doorknob. Peter hid behind his father, hoping no one would answer. But a moment later, there was a shuffling noise. Tattoo opened the door cautiously, not taking off the safety chain.

"Yes?" he croaked through the crack. His face was unshaven, and he squinted out through half-open eyelids.

"Sorry to bother you." Mr. Andersen cleared his throat. "I'm Arne Andersen, and I'm staying here with my wife and kids. Seems there was some question about a key that the kids found in our closet?"

Tattoo scratched his beard for a moment, then broke out in a smile. But he made no move to open his door wider. "The key. Yes, I believe that was all a misunderstanding. A friend of mine thought he lost a key, but, uh, we've located it. Complete misunderstanding. I'm sorry to have bothered your children with such a silly thing."

"Oh, I see." Mr. Andersen took a step back. "I thought it was something like that. Just wanted to make sure. . . ."

"Absolutely." Tattoo kept nodding his head. "I'm so glad you checked. But it was nothing, really. Good day, now."

The door slammed shut in their faces, and Mr. Andersen looked down at Peter.

"Well?" he asked Peter as they walked back to their room.

"Didn't seem like he thought it was such a silly thing yesterday," mumbled Peter.

"Okay, well, I hope that clears things up. Now, I just have a couple of meetings this morning, but I'm taking this afternoon off so we can all go to the palace together. Are you kids going to be okay while we're gone?"

Peter nodded. "We'll be fine."

———

"Okay, okay, I give up. I'll play, I'll play." Peter finally threw up his hands. "Just this once, if she wants to play hide-and-seek so much."

Johanna looked at Elise, who nodded. The little girl broke into a huge smile and jumped up and down. "I'll hide," she squealed, holding her bear tightly. Peter checked to make sure the seam Elise had sewn was holding.

"Okay, Johanna," said Elise. "You and I will hide, and Peter will try to find us. Okay?"

"Only on the ground floor," said Peter. "No going upstairs where we might see those two guys."

Elise frowned. "Don't get started on that again, Peter. We don't want to scare Johanna."

"All right, all right. What do I do—hide my eyes and count to one hundred in German? Let me see, *eins, zwei* . . ."

Elise and Johanna ran out of the room and down the hall while Peter counted as fast as he could.

I should be counting in Danish, he thought. *I forget half the numbers in German.*

" . . . one hundred, ready or not, here I come!"

Peter looked out their hotel door into the quiet hall, feeling a little silly. *What if someone sees us?* he thought, slipping out of their room.

"Elise, you're no good at this," Peter called out to his sister, who was obviously crouching behind a large potted plant at the end of a hallway. "I can see you from here easy. Where's Johanna?"

"She wanted to find her own hiding place," explained Elise, standing up and pointing in the direction Peter had come. "I told her not to go past the lobby."

"She's a funny kid," replied Peter. "First she was scared to go anywhere without holding on to you. Now as soon as we play a game, she wants to go hide by herself."

"I know, it doesn't make sense. Maybe I shouldn't have let her hide."

"It's okay, we'll find her."

Five minutes later, Peter nervously tried to think of any other hiding places they hadn't checked.

"Johanna!" called Elise. "Peter gives up. Johanna!"

"Well, she's not where you told her to stay," said Peter, looking behind a bookshelf in the hotel's reading room. "We've looked everywhere."

He passed a closed door and tried the doorknob. "Hey, what's in here?"

"Peter, maybe it's somebody's room," warned Elise.

"But there's no number on it." Peter gave the door a tug and stepped back. They looked down a rough set of stairs into what was obviously the hotel's basement. A bare lightbulb hung halfway down the stairs, casting a weak pool of light into a dusty storage area full of broken dining room chairs, a mattress, and a stack of boxes. It smelled damp and a little mildewed, but cool and comfortable.

"Johanna?" called Peter. There was no sound in the dark basement, but he thought he could see a faint set of footprints in the dusty stairs. "Johanna?"

A ROYAL VISIT

Peter turned to his sister as they stared down into the shadowy hotel basement. "There's no way Johanna would go down there by herself, is there?"

Elise looked puzzled. "I wouldn't think so. But she's different about this game. I'm not sure."

"Johanna," Peter called once more, starting down the stairs. The back of his neck tingled, and he took a deep breath. "Johanna, this isn't a good place to hide."

"Johanna, please come out if you're down there." Elise followed him.

At the bottom of the stairs Peter heard a small giggle, then a laugh. Johanna jumped out from behind a furnace and waved her arms.

"Aya!" Peter yelled in fright, feeling as if he had just stuck his finger in a light socket.

"You couldn't find me!" Johanna told them, laughing. "I scared you."

Peter and Elise looked at each other and shook their heads.

"Whose idea was this?" asked Peter.

Elise took Johanna by the hand and they turned to go back up the stairway, just as a man stopped at the doorway.

"Uh, could you leave that door open, please?" asked Peter. With the light bulb in his face he couldn't see who was standing there. But then he took another step up and froze. He didn't know whether to hide or keep walking. A man that looked a lot like Mr. Eyebrows stood staring down at the twins and Johanna.

"Who are you talking to, Peter?" asked Elise from behind him. Peter couldn't move, and the man disappeared.

―――――――

"Aren't you excited, Peter?" asked his mother, sitting next to Mr. Andersen on the streetcar. Since it was early afternoon, only a few other people rode with them.

Peter looked away from the half-open window and glanced over at his mother's wristwatch. One-thirty in the afternoon, and the butterflies in his stomach still wouldn't settle down.

"I still don't feel too good," Peter told his mother. He had been afraid to tell his parents about their hide-and-seek game back at the hotel. Afraid to tell them about seeing the man again.

"You'll be fine," replied Mrs. Andersen. "My stomach feels a little nervous, too."

Peter nodded and practiced the line he had been rehearsing for the past few hours, over and over, under his breath. "How do you do, Your Majersty. No, no. Majesty. Maj-es-ty. How do your— no . . ."

"What are you mumbling over there?" asked Elise.

"Nothing," he replied, looking out at the street. They were rolling past one of the giant stone churches they had seen the day before. "Just practicing what I'm going to say."

Their father leaned over with a smile. "I'm going to say, 'Hi, Chris, how are you doing?'"

"Dad!" moaned Elise.

"Just kidding," he assured them.

"What's Johanna going to say?" asked Peter. The little girl smiled up at him.

"She doesn't have to say anything," replied his sister, taking Johanna's hand and standing up. "But this is our stop. Frederik's Church."

Everyone tumbled out the back doors of the tram when they opened, Mr. Andersen in the lead.

"Come on," said Mr. Andersen, already striding off down the sidewalk past the church toward the palace one block away. "We're going to be late."

At the back of the line, Peter tumbled down the two steps to the curb and almost lost his balance. He reached out so he wouldn't fall, grasping for the side of the door. But whatever he grabbed by the doorway felt slippery, and he tumbled.

"Peter," Elise looked back. "Don't fall."

Peter looked up from the sidewalk and scrambled to his feet.

"Not a problem," he said quickly, dusting off his knee.

No one else looked back until they were almost to the palace, a cluster of four tall, square buildings built of sandy gray brick and studded with dozens of tall, white-paned windows. It wasn't a typical fairy-tale castle—no Cinderella towers or moats—but Peter thought the four palaces were still very grand. They were nearly identical, and they all had a balcony in the middle, up high, framed by three tall glass doors. That was where the king and queen could come out and wave at people. Below that balcony was a huge square, or plaza, big enough to hold ten thousand people shoulder to shoulder for things like the king's birthday or Constitution Day.

Four streets led out of the corners of the square, evenly dividing the four palaces and the smaller, shorter add-on buildings that gave each of the lofty palace buildings a set of shoulders. In the middle stood another king-on-a-horse statue, a lot like the one in front of their hotel.

It's either Christian something or Frederik something, Peter told himself, smiling as he stared at the statue. Of course, by tradition, those were the only two names Danish kings had been given for over four hundred years.

"Okay, does everyone look presentable?" asked Mrs. Andersen. She turned around to inspect the kids. Johanna was shining in her new red dress with white lace trim. Elise had fixed the little girl's golden hair into two matching ponytails.

Elise herself looked ready for church, too, with her own blue-and-white flowered knee-length dress. But Mrs. Andersen's eyes grew wide when she stopped to look at Peter.

"Oh, Peter, what happened to you?" she croaked.

"What do you mean?" asked Peter, looking down. Then he saw the black, greasy fingerprints streaked all over the front of his starched white shirt, mostly around his pocket.

"Oh no," moaned Elise. "Leave it to Peter to get messed up—"

"Elise, I couldn't help it," replied Peter. "It must have been from the tram, when I fell. I told you I should have stayed at the hotel."

"Well, it's too late now." Mr. Andersen stepped up to Peter and tried to wipe off the worst of the grime. He only succeeded in smudging the grease around.

"Arne, I am not bringing this child in to see the king of Denmark," insisted Mrs. Andersen, looking around the square to see if anyone had noticed them. "He looks like he just crawled out from underneath a bus!"

"Take it easy, Karen," replied Mr. Andersen, wiping the sweat off his forehead.

"Mom, it's fine." Peter attempted to hide the worst grease smudge with his hand, while his mother took a handkerchief and tried to wipe it clean. She shook her head.

"This is not going to work, Arne," she said through tight lips.

Elise and Johanna giggled at the sight of Peter getting a cat bath in the royal square. Peter just made a face at them and pretended to look as if he didn't notice any of the attention. Mrs. Andersen frowned.

"This is not funny, girls," she told them.

"Sorry," said Elise, putting her hand up to cover a grin.

"Here," said Mr. Andersen. "I have an idea. Peter, give me your knife. I hope it's sharp."

He took Peter's pocketknife, opened up the blade, and carefully began to carve the threads that held Peter's pocket. A moment later, he yanked off the grease-stained pocket.

"There!" he said. "Good as new. Or at least, better than before."

Peter looked down at his shirt. There were just a few threads where the pocket had been, but at least the greasy hand print was gone. His mother just shook her head. Then Mr. Andersen looked at his watch once more.

"Now we really are late," he said, replacing his handkerchief in his coat pocket. "But that's as good as you're going to get, Peter. Maybe you could walk backward to meet the king."

"Or turn your shirt inside out," suggested Elise, grinning.

"Now that's an idea," answered Peter, following his parents once more. This time they marched right through the crowds of tourists in front of the main palace building, up to a phone-booth-sized guardhouse where a red-suited guard with a tall, dark beaver-skin hat stood stiffly at attention.

"What do you think we'll need to do to get him to talk?" Peter whispered to Elise. They looked at their father.

But no one needed to find out. Just as Mr. Andersen was clearing his throat to talk to the guard, a pleasant-looking girl in her late teens stepped out of the front door of the palace. She caught their eye and looked questioningly at Mrs. Andersen, who was closest to her.

"You look like you might be the Andersens," she said with a bright smile. "I've been keeping my eye out for a lost-looking family with two children."

"That's us," answered Mr. Andersen, looking relieved that he didn't have to talk his way into the palace past any guard. "But we have three children . . . actually, I—"

"Three?" The girl looked down at a clipboard in her hand,

then looked from face to face. "Well, I recognize Peter and Elise from your picture in the newspaper. But—"

"This is Johanna," put in Mrs. Andersen. "She's a refugee orphan from Germany, and, ah—"

"It's kind of a long story," interrupted Peter. Mrs. Andersen gave him a look that told him he should keep his mouth shut.

"Yes, Peter's right," continued their mother. "It is a bit of a long story. But it turns out that we're taking care of her for a few days. I hope it's all right that we brought her along."

Johanna seemed to know that people were talking about her. She smiled and held up her bear for everyone to see.

"Alfred," said Johanna, as if it were a special introduction.

"Oh, of course." The girl smiled broadly, then shook hands with everyone—including the bear. "There's plenty of room in the palace for Alfred, too. By the way, I'm Susanne Elvstrom, a page here at the palace. Kind of an errand girl."

Peter thought she looked more like a college student than a page in Denmark's royal court, with a businesslike skirt and some of the whitest teeth Peter could ever remember seeing. Her light brown hair was cut short, and she stood almost as tall as their father. She smiled again as she turned to open a tall, dark metal door leading into the building.

"King Christian has asked me to help you find your way around the palace."

Susanne motioned for them to follow while stone-faced guards held their rifles stiffly out in front and stood aside. They wore royal red jackets with black pants, white belts, and white gloves. Their tall fur hats almost made them look like giants. Peter felt like saluting, but he forgot all about the outside of the palace as soon as they stepped inside.

As the door clanged shut behind them, the street sounds faded away. Elise gasped when she saw the room they were standing in.

"It's beautiful," she whispered, and even her whisper seemed to echo. "Like we're dolls in a dollhouse. Everything's so big."

Peter looked at his reflection in the polished marble floor. "Nice and cool in here. Even better than the hotel."

Everyone else stared in wonder around them at the magnificent life-sized paintings of kings and queens, the high ceilings, the huge red velvet curtains around the windows. Susanne waited for them to look around, as if she was used to having people do the same thing when they stepped inside.

"This is King Christian's residence palace, where the royal family lives," she told them. "Queen Alexandrine lives here, too, of course, but she's on a trip to the country until tomorrow. Prince Knud and Crown Prince Frederik live here with their families, as well."

"Will we see the princesses?" asked Elise. Her voice echoed up to the tall ceiling and back down.

Susanne smiled. "Margrethe and Benedicte went with their grandmother, so I'm afraid they aren't in the palace today. So I think the king would like some company. Here, follow me, please."

As they walked down grand halls filled with paintings, Peter tried to keep his feet from clicking on the polished floors. He wasn't as disappointed as Elise seemed that the little princesses were gone. Susanne gave them a running history lesson of the palace.

"All four buildings were built between 1749 and 1760," she told them. "But they didn't become a home for kings until a few years later, in 1794, when the other palace, the Christiansborg Palace, burned."

The history lesson came to an end when they stopped in front of an oak-paneled door at the end of a hall.

"This is King Christian's study, where he likes to spend most of his time." She lowered her voice and checked her watch. "He should be ready for you."

At Susanne's knock, there was a friendly "Come in!" and the aide cautiously pushed the door open.

"The Andersens here to see you, Your Majesty."

Peter whispered his lines once again under his breath. "How do you do, Your Highjesty—"

A moment later they were standing awkwardly in the king's office. The wood-paneled walls were covered with small, framed photos—mostly of people on horses—and several tall bookshelves were filled with worn, mismatched books. The room had the comfortable, lived-in smell of leather chairs, books, and coffee.

The king's midsized carved walnut desk was also comfortably cluttered with papers, the morning newspaper, and several books. Peter recognized an open Bible on top of all the papers. And behind the desk sat King Christian.

He was just like the photos. Like a kindly grandfather. The king was in his early seventies, but he seemed strong and young. His hair was combed neatly back, and a silvery gray mustache could only partly hide a broad grin. Nothing hid the sparkle of his bright gray eyes as he looked up at his visitors.

"Please excuse me for not standing," he apologized. "I'm afraid my leg is still a little weak after I hurt it in my riding accident."

One by one they each got to shake his hand. When it came time for his turn, Peter tried to remember what he was going to say. As he feared, his mind went completely blank.

"Uh . . . I'm . . ." He fumbled for words, but his tongue refused to obey. "This is . . ."

He looked over at Elise, and for a moment he couldn't seem to remember even his own name.

"That's Elise," he finally managed. Of course, Elise had already been introduced. Peter's ears turned fire-engine red, and they felt as if they were steaming.

"You must be Peter," said the king, smiling kindly. He looked casual in his plain short-sleeved shirt and riding pants. "Quite a good photo of you and your sister in the paper this morning. Did you see it?"

Peter shook his head and managed to squeak out a "No, sir,"

while the king rummaged around on his desk until he found the front page of the paper.

"Front page, even," said King Christian, pointing to the black-and-white photo of Peter and Elise smiling nervously at the camera. "Nice article, too. But sit down, all of you, relax, and we can chat a little. Coffee?"

Susanne disappeared to fetch a tray of coffee while the king asked them several easy questions about their home and school. But he wasn't at all like Peter thought he was going to be. Mostly he talked just like their grandfather Andersen. Warm, relaxed, and with a touch of humor.

"I've never heard a story quite like yours," he told them, leaning forward with his hands folded over his desk. "Tell me more about how you made it across to Sweden with your friend . . . what was his name?"

"Henrik, sir," answered Elise.

"Yes, Henrik. I was glad that so many of our Jewish friends made it to safety. Even more glad that they're all coming home. But I understand Henrik's father is not well?"

Elise told the king about Henrik's father, and after more questions, she and Peter ended up telling many of their adventures from the past few years. Susanne returned with a tray full of steaming coffee, watered down with loads of cream and sugar for the kids. Behind her, a maid came with trays of tea biscuits and little pastries. Mrs. Andersen smiled and nodded when the twins looked over at her, so Peter took a good handful of biscuits.

All the while the king leaned forward in his chair, his bright eyes blazing with interest. Once in a while he would shake his head in wonder, or click his tongue and sip his coffee.

"And here you are—1945 and you're sitting safely in the royal palace," he said finally, after the twins had told their stories for at least fifteen minutes. "How do you account for that?"

Peter was caught off guard by the question.

"How?" asked Peter, confused.

"Yes," replied the king, a smile playing at his lips. "How do you explain to people how you made it safely through so many fantastic adventures? People must ask you, do they not? It sounds like something out of a storybook."

Peter was afraid to say the obvious, but the king seemed to be waiting for an answer to his question. Elise cleared her throat.

"Peter doesn't always say so, Your Majesty," she said finally, "but we were both praying the whole way across the water to Sweden. And we know God got us out of the submarine, too." Elise looked over at her brother and continued. "God really answered our prayers."

The king smiled and nodded. "I was hoping you would say something like that. Reminds me of the Bible verse I was reading just before you arrived." Then he closed his eyes, remembering. For a moment it was very much as if Grandfather Andersen were sitting in front of them, rather than the king of Denmark.

"'I know that you have little strength,'" quoted the king, "'yet you have kept my word and have not denied my name.' That's Revelation three-something. I don't recall the verse. But it's there on the right side of the page."

He turned to his open Bible, which was lying next to the newspaper, and put on his glasses once more. "Three . . ." He ran his finger down the page, then flipped through a few pages. "Verse eight." He folded his glasses and leaned back in his chair, the same way Grandfather Andersen would. Then he chuckled. "Maybe I should have been a pastor. But my father had other ideas for my future."

Peter wasn't sure if he should laugh at the joke. Susanne did, though—a light, easy laugh that made them all relax.

"Well, but I'm tired of sitting," continued King Christian, putting down his coffee. "I have something I'd like to show you two that I think you might be interested in." He looked over at their parents. "That is, if your parents and little Johanna here wouldn't mind having Susanne show them around a little more?"

"Anything you want to do is fine with us," answered Mr. Andersen.

"Ah yes." King Christian nodded and pushed his wheelchair away from his desk. "I'll just need a little help."

Peter took the back of the wheelchair, wondering how he had come to be in this position.

"Don't worry about your parents," the king joked over his shoulder. "They'll be fine. And I'll show you where to go. Now, down this hallway, second door on the right."

The King's Secret

Peter and Elise looked curiously at each other, but neither dared ask where they were going. Elise held the door open as they wheeled the king into a smaller, empty room that looked as if it were used as a small library.

"This is for staff," explained the king. "People who work here. But over here is what I want to show you."

King Christian pointed at the carved panels of a wall, but Peter couldn't see anything else.

"That's right," said the king. "The wall. Here, wheel me over there and I'll have you two help me."

Peter did as he was told, and they helped the king to his feet next to the wall. He stood unsteadily at first, then straightened out. But still the king limped on his bad foot as he stepped up to the wall.

"Here," commanded the king. "Pull this handle with me."

Again the twins obeyed, and all three pulled at a small door-sized panel that opened to reveal a short stairway down to a dark, musty tunnel. The king looked at them with a smile.

"This is what I wanted to show you. All kids like secret tunnels, right?"

Peter couldn't believe what he was seeing.

"Wow," he whispered, and his whisper seemed to echo.

The king held up his finger. "The only thing I have to ask is that you keep this tunnel a secret. I had it built during the war years, and the Germans never found out. We were going to use it if there ever came a serious emergency."

"Did you ever use it?" asked Elise.

"Not because I had to. Only to get out of a boring meeting once." He chuckled. "But how about it? Is it our secret?"

Peter nodded, then realized that nobody could see him in the dark.

"Absolutely," Peter promised, and Elise agreed.

"Good. Now you young people will have to excuse me, but I'm going to be a little slow. If I could just hold on to one of you on the way down, I'll be just fine."

The king produced a small flashlight, and as they entered the tunnel Peter touched the beams along the walls.

"It's quite safe," the king assured them. "I had some of our best engineers build it." He chuckled again. "The only thing was, they didn't make it quite high enough for me to stand up in."

Peter smiled as he breathed in the cool, damp air that smelled like a garden at night. The tunnel wasn't long—twenty paces into the darkness with two turns. Soon the king stopped at the bottom of a set of steep stairs, almost like the one they had climbed down.

"Here's where I need your help again, young people." The king pointed his flashlight at the ceiling, where soft sunlight filtered through the cracks of a wooden door. "If one of you could open that door, we'll all go see what's upstairs."

Elise and Peter both crawled up, pushed up on the door, and almost fell out on the swept floor of a large stable. It smelled of fresh hay and horses, and Peter blinked for a minute at the two rows of large animals. Then he remembered who was still down in the tunnel.

"Can I help you, Your Majesty?"

King Christian was already struggling up the steep set of stairs, one at a time.

"Thank you, kids," he puffed. "I may be an old man, and my leg may not work the way it used to, but I can still manage."

He smiled broadly as he straightened up inside the stable.

"That's better," he told them as he shuffled slowly over to a tall gray horse, backed into a trim, whitewashed stall. He leaned on a railing for balance, under a set of saddles hanging on the wall. "The palace is nice, but this is my favorite place."

"Where are we?" asked Peter, looking around at the saddles and bridles hanging on the wall.

"This is what we call the old Queen's Stable," replied King Christian. Peter and Elise followed him over to the horse, which was already saddled. "It's not the main stable, but in the old days one of the queens wanted a place a little closer to home where she could keep a couple of animals. I think it was a good idea. Just thirty meters and across Frederik's Street from my palace over there."

Peter looked in the direction the king had pointed, trying to get his bearings.

"I can see why this is your favorite place," said Elise quietly, stroking the horse's long, dappled gray-and-white neck.

"You like horses?" asked King Christian, smiling.

Elise nodded her head. "Peter and I rode ponies once on the coast. When we were little. But they weren't as big as this."

"Well, I've got a couple of ponies," the king smiled. "A gift from the Norwegians for the princesses a couple of years ago. They'll have to grow into them, though." He looked around and pointed down the corridor.

"Peter, go down to the last stall and bring back the tan pony. He should be saddled and waiting if the stable hand did what I asked. And Elise, the other pony is probably in the stall across the corridor. There are some riding clothes you can change into, as well. Go and see, and then bring her back here, would you?"

The twins hurried to obey—and Peter wondered what was happening.

"Are we really going to go riding?" Peter asked his sister.

Elise gave him a hopeful look, as if she wasn't sure what to believe. "That's what it looks like. But where would we go?"

They found the two ponies in stalls as the king had told them. Carefully, Peter unlatched the gate and reached in to untie the small pony's reins from the side railing. And as the king had said, someone had already saddled the animals.

"Down here." The king motioned for them to hurry. "I don't want anyone to come before we leave."

"Um, Your Majesty," said Elise, holding the reins of her pony. The yellow blouse and black riding pants she had found were just a bit too large. "Does this mean that we should go riding with you?"

The king laughed. "I'm sorry. I've involved you in this plot, but I haven't told you yet what we're doing! I've been waiting for three years to ride through the streets of the city once more. The doctors tell me not to. Prince Frederik begs me not to. Queen Alexandrine says she forbids it. But now is my chance. Maybe my last chance to ride through the streets, the way I used to every day during the war. And you're going to help me."

"Yes, sir." Peter smiled. "What do you want us to do?"

"Fetch that stepladder." The king pointed behind one of the stalls. "And my jacket is hanging right over there. Elise, you help me open this stall and get Jubilee out. I'm going to need some help climbing up. Once I'm up there, I'll be all right."

It took a few minutes, but finally they got the large gray horse out of the stall, turned around, and standing still so the king could climb on. Peter pulled up the stepladder and gave King Christian a shoulder to lean on while he climbed each step. Then the king sat down on the top of the ladder and swung his good right leg over the horse.

"That's a good boy, Jubilee," said the king. He slid sideways into the saddle with a satisfied grunt.

The king turned to Peter with a smile. "I have to tell you, I've been waiting for this moment for three years. Jubilee is a good horse—a present for my seventieth birthday, you know. It's just that someone spooked him on that birthday ride and he threw me. Perhaps you remember that."

Peter nodded. The entire country of Denmark remembered the day when King Christian's horse ran out of control down the streets of Copenhagen, and the king was thrown to the cobblestone street. Their beloved king had almost died.

And here I am, helping him to get back into the saddle of the same horse, thought Peter.

"Don't worry, Peter." The king winked. "If anybody asks, I'll be sure to tell them it was all my fault." He straightened up in the saddle and gripped the reins. "But after all, I'm still king."

"Yes, sir," agreed Elise as she closed the gate to Jubilee's stall. "Would you like me to open the door out to the plaza?"

The king was about to answer when a rear door swung open and a young man dressed in work clothes stepped in, whistling. He stopped short when he saw the king on Jubilee, and his mouth dropped open.

"Your Majesty," said the boy, who looked about the same age as Susanne from the palace. "I thought the saddles were for someone else. The queen said—"

"Never mind the queen," roared King Christian. "I'm going riding with my two young friends here. Get on your pony, Elise. Jens is going to open the outside door for us."

But the stable hand stood still, looking amazed.

"A fly is going to find its way into your mouth if you don't close it soon, Jens. And would you please open the door?"

It was a command no one could ignore. Jens jumped to attention, snapped his mouth shut, and ran over to the large double doors to pull the bars away. Then he swung the doors open to the courtyard.

"Let's go for a ride, you two. Just stay behind me. The ponies are used to following." He made a sound with his lips, and the royal-looking horse gently led the way outside. Peter saluted the stable hand as they passed by.

"Thanks," said Peter, all smiles. He was last in line behind Elise, and he wasn't sure how to make his pony go. But it seemed to know the way in their little parade.

"Hey, this is easy," said Peter. "The ponies just kind of drive themselves, huh?"

"Just give them their reins," the king coached them over his shoulder. "Don't hold back on the reins too tightly. They're used to following me. Won't the newspaper reporters get a kick out of this!"

Outside, Peter could see the usual crowds of tourists and city people, some walking around in the late-morning sun, looking at the four matching palaces. Others were standing in clusters, watching the guards and taking pictures. But everything stopped as the people heard the triple clip-clop of the animals' hooves.

Even the guards turned their heads, and Peter could see their wide-eyed amazement at the sight of King Christian on Jubilee leading two kids out of the royal stable on ponies. Everything in the huge courtyard square fell silent, except for hooves on the ancient cobblestones. But then someone yelled the announcement: "It's King Christian! King Christian is on his horse again!"

The yell was like a signal as everyone in the square hurried to line a pathway on either side of the king. Peter felt his pony hesitate at the sound of the yelling, but he tapped his heels lightly against the pony's side, the way he had read cowboys did it in America.

"King Christian! You're back on your horse!" someone yelled.

From high up on his horse, King Christian smiled and nodded at the people. He also kept a watchful eye on Peter and Elise, who were lagging behind.

"Are you two with me?" he called back over the cheers of the crowd.

"Right behind you, Your Majesty," said Peter, giving his pony another gentle tap with his heels.

People everywhere! They hung out of windows four stories up on either side of the street, and they roared their happiness to see the old king out on his horse one more time. Many waved flags, the same way Peter had seen when the Danish troops came back on the day after the war had ended.

From somewhere high above, a group of people leaned out their window and began to sing, and soon everyone on the street joined in a mass chorus of "King Christian Stood by the High Mast," one of Denmark's national songs. The words echoed up and down the street:

"King Christian stood by the tall, tall mast in smoke and mist . . ."

The song was written about another King Christian hundreds of years before that. But the people only sang louder and louder, as if it were written just for their king.

"Who stands against King Christian in battle?" echoed the words to the song, and Peter had to sing along. His pony held up to wait for Elise's while the crowds milled around the king and cheered.

"I hope the king's horse doesn't get scared again," said Elise over the crowd.

"Me too," said Peter. He gave his pony a gentle tap with his heels, but the two animals seemed happy just to walk together.

"I think this pony is going his own speed," Peter told his sister.

"I can't make mine go any faster either."

Up ahead, people still pressed in around the king and his horse, and Peter looked around at the faces. Everyone seemed as if they were at a New Year's party, or better. Then one middle-aged man took a step out in front of them, looked back, and froze for a moment when he saw Peter and Elise on their ponies.

"Well, would you look at that," said the man, a bright smile spreading out below one of the largest noses Peter had ever seen. "Peter and Elise Andersen. Riding horses with the king, now, are you?"

"Pastor Kai!" said Elise, pulling her pony up beside Peter's.

"How are you? I mean, what are you doing here? We haven't seen you since last summer."

Their friend walked over to the ponies and gave the twins each a kind of hug, or as much as he could manage with them in the saddle.

"Well, since you didn't come to see your cousins on the farm this year, I thought I'd come try to find *you*. Our little country church was kind of quiet without the Andersen twins visiting."

They all laughed, and he continued.

"No, I'm just kidding you. Actually, I'm here in the city for a couple of days helping a young fellow with some . . . well, mostly paper work. In fact . . ." He looked at his wristwatch. "He's probably waiting for me. But where are your parents?"

Elise pointed back at the palace. "They're still getting a tour. King Christian sent us an invitation to come visit him and everything!"

By that time the king was far ahead, surrounded by crowds. Pastor Kai shook his head and smiled.

"I've read all the articles about you two. It's all in our local paper. Your cousins are keeping a scrapbook. And they keep asking your aunt and uncle when you're coming to visit the farm again."

"It seems so long ago since we visited their farm," said Peter.

"Doesn't it?" agreed Pastor Kai. He looked at his watch once more. "What a crazy place to meet two of my favorite twelve-year-olds. God must be doing something special again. Look, where are you staying?"

"The Hotel d'Angleterre," replied Elise, trying to hold her pony back as it edged forward. Pastor Kai raised his eyebrows, and he reminded Peter once more of a pleasant, absentminded professor.

"First class, eh?"

"Dad's boss was supposed to come," explained Elise, "but then he got sick. So the bank paid to have Dad come instead, and we got to come with him."

Pastor Kai nodded. "Well, listen, I'll let you get back to your ride. But after I finish up my business here—probably tomorrow, or maybe the next day—I'll call you at the hotel, okay?"

By that time Peter's pony couldn't wait any longer but set out at a trot through the crowd to catch up with the king's horse. Peter grabbed a handful of the pony's cream-colored mane and held on. "Sounds great!" he called over his shoulder as people looked up in surprise and jumped out of the way.

"Coming through!" yelled Peter.

"What a crazy place to meet Pastor Kai again," said Elise when her pony had again caught up to Peter's.

"Yeah," agreed Peter, trying to navigate through the crowd. The closer they got to the king, the thicker it got. "What did he say he was doing way over here on the other side of the country?"

Elise wrinkled her forehead. "Something about helping a guy with paper work? I'm not sure."

"Well, you remember Pastor Kai," said Peter, thinking back to the time they had spent with the man the summer before when they had visited their cousins' sheep ranch. "He was always running out of the house, helping people with something."

"Well, there you are," boomed King Christian when they had finally caught up. "I thought maybe you were leaving me to finish the ride by myself."

"Oh no, sir," replied Peter, trying to talk above the noise of the crowd. "We just ran into a pastor friend of ours from over on the coast."

"Kind of a friend of the family," added Elise.

The king nodded. "I see. Well, ready to ride on?"

A little man with a large camera hanging from his neck stepped out of the crowd before they could get their horses moving again.

"Hey, kids, how about a snapshot of you and King Christian?"

It wasn't the sort of question that waited for an answer. The man just raised the camera to his eye and stepped back a few steps, behind Peter and Elise, off into the crowd a bit. Someone cheered from the balcony above their heads.

"Big smiles," said the photographer. "This is for *The Times*."

While the photographer was adjusting his camera, Peter's pony started to wander off to the left. He reached for the reins on that side, missed grabbing them, and somehow lost his balance. The next moment, Peter was sliding sideways off his seat, head-first, right into the arms of a mailman in a red jacket.

"What?" laughed the mailman, holding Peter up as he got to his feet. "That's a different way to get off your pony."

Peter looked around for only a second, trying to figure out what had happened. He swung back into the saddle as the crowd around him laughed.

"Thanks," mumbled Peter, his face as red as the mailman's jacket. The photographer snapped a few more photos and waved his hand. "That was great," he told them, rolling the film on his camera. "Especially the somersault by the kid. Great."

Yeah, great, thought Peter, looking around nervously. *One more newspaper picture, but in this one I'm standing on my head, looking like a clown.*

Peter tried not to look around at the giggling people and slapped the reins on his pony's cream-colored mane. "Let's go, horsey."

The king chose a route down one street and around a block as the streets filled with more and more people.

"What time is it?" asked Peter as they bumped along.

Elise looked around the crowd and shrugged. "We've been out about a half-hour. Why?"

Peter stood up in his stirrups. "I don't know. I guess I'm not used to this trail riding."

"Trail riding!" Elise laughed. "The Wild West of Copenhagen!"

Up ahead, King Christian still sat with his back as straight as a board. But even he teetered once in a while, and Peter wondered how the older man was doing. As they rounded the last corner back to the royal square, Peter could see faces in the palace windows, up on the second floor.

"Look, Elise," he called back over his shoulder, careful this time not to lean too far. "Mom and Dad are looking out through those windows."

Peter and Elise waved as they got closer, and their parents waved back—maybe with a little less excitement.

"Back to the stable," said the king, clicking his tongue. He pointed Jubilee toward the double doors acrosss the street from the palace. Without a word from anyone, the doors opened just as they approached.

"Thank you, Jens." The king nodded at his stable hand as they rode back into the cool shadows of the stable.

Peter looked over at the king, who was smiling broadly as he slid off the side of his horse. The old king slipped a little when he got to the floor, but Jens kept him from falling.

"Thank you so much for riding with me," he told them, taking their hands. "That was the best ride I've had since my accident. Of course, it's been the only ride since then, but still, it was wonderful. Great to be back on Jubilee." He gave his horse a slap on the back. "No matter what the newspapers said about you after our accident, old boy, you're a fine animal."

"And speaking of newspapers, sir," said Jens, supporting the king's arm, "I saw plenty of reporters out there by the end of your ride. I'm sure we'll make the front pages in the morning."

The king shook his head and brushed off his sleeve. "Ah, that makes me feel a little guilty. I knew we might attract attention, but I can never get used to how quickly those newspaper reporters follow us. Maybe they don't have anything else to write about, now that the war is over."

"Of course, sir," continued Jens. "The queen will be quite worried when she finds out you were riding—especially after the threats to your life last week."

"Foolishness," grunted the king. "I will not hide inside this palace any longer. It's as simple as that! My people are out there. All that nonsense about a German plot to end my life is just a lot of hot air."

"Yes, sir." Jens led Jubilee back into his stall and brought out a brush for the animal. "I'm sure it is."

"I hope we're not in trouble with your parents," said King Christian.

"Oh no, sir," answered Elise. "I'm sure they didn't mind."

Peter tied his pony's reins to a railing. "It was more fun riding with you than anything else."

The king smiled. "A few more rides and you'll be an old pro. And maybe you could teach me how to slide off upside down, the way you did out there." He winked at Peter. "Oh, and by the way, I hope we'll see you at the awards banquet Saturday evening? Six o'clock. The American General Eisenhower himself is going to be there. I'll make sure that you get an official invitation. Now let's get you back to your parents."

Peter and Elise could hardly contain their excitement as they followed the king back through the secret tunnel.

"General Eisenhower!" whispered Elise. "Do you think we'll get to meet him?"

"Sure. The American war hero! Why not?"

They arrived back at the king's study just as their parents and Johanna were coming down the hallway with Susanne. Johanna ran up to Elise as if they had been apart for days. The king extended his invitation to Peter and Elise's parents for the awards banquet, and thanked them for allowing him to take their children on a horseback ride. He then excused himself, and Susanne ushered the family back out to the front entrance.

"You kids are quite the lucky ones," Mrs. Andersen told them as they all stepped out into the royal square. "But I'm afraid you made Johanna terribly jealous."

Elise gulped. "Oh, Mom, I forgot all about that."

"That's all right," replied Elise's mother. "It's just that, well, as soon as she found out what you were doing, she wanted to go for a pony ride with the king, too."

Elise looked down at Johanna with a smile. "Oh, I'm sorry, Johanna. We didn't know what King Christian was doing, or we would have brought you along."

"Next time?" asked Johanna.

Elise just smiled.

"Your mom's right about being lucky," said Susanne. "No one else has ever been able to ride with the king like that. But I'll tell you, it's a good thing Queen Alexandrine is away for a couple of days. She would never have let him go!"

JOHANNA IS MISSING

"Now, are you sure you two will be okay staying here again with little Johanna?" Mrs. Andersen nervously stepped into a pair of high-heeled shoes and looked at her lipstick once more in the mirror over the sink in their hotel room.

"Don't worry about us, Mom." Elise sat on the edge of the bed. "I've been a babysitter before."

Mrs. Andersen lowered her voice and leaned down to her daughter. "It's not you I'm worried about," she whispered. "You just need to keep an eye on your brother."

"I heard that," said Peter, who was combing his hair by the mirror. "You just go with Dad to your breakfast, or lunch, or whatever it is. We're getting used to it."

"It's a brunch, and I'm only going down for the first part with your father. It's right here in this building, in the little restaurant we were in before, so I'm not far away. I'm just sorry to leave you again."

"We're fine, Mom, really." Elise stood up and straightened out her dress. "We'll take care of Johanna."

"All right." Mrs. Andersen blew them all a kiss as she walked out the door. "When I get back in an hour we'll go do something fun. Just stay in the building."

"Of course, Mom," said Peter, leaning out the door and watching his mother disappear down the hall. When she was gone, he turned back to his sister and Johanna, who were looking out the window.

Now's my chance, he thought. "I'll be right back," he told them, opening the door.

"Remember what Mom said about staying in the building," Elise called after him.

"Yes, Mom," he answered.

I have to find out what they're up to, Peter told himself, slipping quietly down a hallway. No one was around except for the morning maids, who were making beds and rolling their carts down the hall. He climbed the big stairway and made his way down the second-floor hallway.

"Let's see," he whispered, following the numbers on the doors. "Here's Room 20, 21 . . ."

Peter looked hopefully up and down the hallway, waiting for one of the maids to come with her fresh sheets. He thought he caught a whiff of bleach or some kind of cleaner. *They must be close by. Maybe if I'm just walking past when they're making the beds, I can see inside.*

Peter stopped in front of the room with the "Do Not Disturb" sign just as Elise and Johanna showed up at the far end of the hall. Johanna let out a shout.

"Hey, Peter!" she yelled, skipping down the wood floor. "What are you doing up here?"

Peter put a finger to his lips and waved his other hand for her to slow down. "Shh!"

Johanna stopped, puzzled. Peter motioned for them to come, and pointed to the room.

"Quiet," he whispered. Johanna seemed to understand, even though he was speaking in Danish. Elise tiptoed up to where they were standing.

"This is the room where Mr. Eyebrows is," he told them as a phone rang from inside the room. Peter jumped, then looked around nervously to see if anyone would hear.

"Just the phone," whispered Elise as it rang once more. Peter put his ear up to the keyhole as someone answered the phone.

"Peter," whispered Elise, pulling back on his shirt, "you're being too snoopy."

Peter put up his hand, trying to hear what was being said. "We have to find out what this guy is up to."

Elise folded her arms and looked up and down the halls. From inside the room a man's voice mumbled something, then laughed.

It sounds like German, thought Peter. He motioned for Johanna to listen.

"German?" he whispered into the little girl's ear. Johanna leaned closer to the door and smiled.

"Ja, ist Deutsch," she said in her regular voice. "It's German."

Peter put his hand to her mouth as the man inside Room 22 laughed once more.

"Of course the plan is going to work," said the voice inside the room, a little louder. By that time Elise had stooped down to hear what was going on, too.

"I already told you not to worry," continued the man's voice. "I know you wanted the key . . . yes, but if you were a better pickpocket you wouldn't have any problem. But see, we don't need it now to get inside."

There was a moment of silence as the person on the other end of the line talked.

"Right. Trust me, will you? This is the way the general wanted us to do it. It was his last command, and I am going to carry it out, whether you help me or—"

Another pause.

"All right, all right. Work it out with the kid and I'll see you back here. We still have time to finish before Saturday night. Heil Hitler!"

That was all Peter and Elise needed to hear. Peter grabbed Johanna by the hand and ran, trying his best not to make any noise. Elise was right beside him as they dove around the corner of the hallway.

Looking back toward Room 22, Peter could tell the door had opened. They held their breath and slowly backed away down the rest of the hall, toward the stairway which would take them safely down to the lobby.

"That was close, Peter," said Elise when they were finally back in their own room. She leaned against the door and bolted the lock, breathing hard.

"Did you catch everything he was saying?" asked Peter, pulling down the shade.

"What are you doing that for?" asked his sister.

Peter shrugged. "I don't know. Same reason you just locked the door."

Johanna looked from one twin to the other. "Was that someone we know?"

Elise shook her head. "No, Johanna. We're just being silly. You don't need to worry about a thing."

Peter threw up his hands and bounced on the bed. "How can we tell her that, Elise? You heard what the guy was saying, the 'Heil Hitler' thing. That means these guys are up to something terrible. And it's going to happen Saturday night!"

"I wonder what he meant about the general's last command?" wondered Elise.

Peter jumped off the bed like a rocket when someone rapped on the door. He looked at his sister with wide eyes, wondering what to do.

"You open it," she whispered.

"No, you." Peter slipped quietly up to the door. He gripped the door handle and hesitated.

"Are you kids in there?" asked their mother, knocking once more.

"Oh, Mom, it's just you," said Peter, feeling a wave of relief as he unbolted and opened the door.

Mrs. Andersen stood at the doorway, looking amused. "Well, who did you think?"

"Are you back already?" asked Elise. "It's only been forty-five minutes."

Mrs. Andersen looked at the three of them and laughed. "I had a cup of coffee with your father, and then those bank men started talking about money. So I left early."

"Does that mean we're going out to see something else now?" asked Elise, looking eager.

"Put your shoes on," she told them, sounding like a coach about to send her team out on the playing field. She looked down at their feet. "Oh, I see you kids already have your shoes on. Well, okay, it's still not eleven o'clock yet. Let me get out of these heels, and we'll go have some fun!"

"I thought you said we were going to have some fun," complained Peter, dragging his heels past another department store in the bustling downtown area. "We've been shopping all day."

"I'm sorry, Peter," apologized his mother. "I know an hour and a half seems like all day to you. But we just have to find something fancier for little Johanna to wear if she's going to come along with us to the palace tomorrow night. And I didn't want to leave you alone again."

Peter nodded. But he knew he would scream if they dragged him inside one more building that smelled like jasmine perfume and frilly things. Even Johanna looked like she was dragging. Elise gave him a strange look.

"What's that sound?" she asked him.

"That's my stomach. I haven't had anything since that little sandwich at noon."

"Well, it's only one," replied his sister, looking at the window of yet another store. "What about in here, Mom?"

Mrs. Andersen looked at Peter as he leaned against a lamp-post.

"Besides," he told her, "it's hot."

"Okay, Peter, I'll make you a deal," said Mrs. Andersen. "We'll make this the last clothing store for a while if you'll just keep an eye on Johanna while we're inside. If there's anything that might fit her, I'll send Elise out."

Peter opened his eyes. He heard the first part about the "last clothing store" and straightened up.

"What?" he asked as a noisy streetcar clattered past. But he didn't wait for an answer. "Oh yeah, sure." A minute later he looked around to find Johanna gone, and then he realized what his mother had asked him.

"Did she say I was supposed to watch Johanna?" he asked himself. A woman walking by glanced up as if he had asked her the question.

"Hey, excuse me, did you see a little girl run off down the street or something?" he asked her. The lady shook her head and marched on.

Peter looked both ways down the street, then asked a couple of people stopped on their bicycles.

"Sorry," said a woman, shaking her head.

"Oh, Johanna, where did you go?" Peter ran out into the middle of the street, dodging bicycles and cars, ignoring the shouts and the honking horns.

"Get out of the street, kid!" growled a man in a truck as he rumbled by in a cloud of black smoke. Peter could only hold up his hands in a kind of apology. He looked down the street first one direction, then the other.

"There she is!" he said, catching sight of what looked like Johanna's yellow blouse. She was about a block away and running as fast as she could, the same way Peter remembered her doing back when they had found her in the train station. In the distance, Peter could see her darting around bicycles and people on the sidewalk.

"Johanna!" Peter shouted, knowing she couldn't hear him. He started sprinting down the middle of the street, right down the painted yellow line. Cars honked and swerved to avoid him, but Peter kept running.

"Johanna!" he yelled again as he got closer to where he had seen her last. "Oh, come on, Johanna, where do you think you're going?"

"Hey, what's wrong with the sidewalk?" shouted another driver. Peter couldn't look, only kept running.

A block later, Peter finally ran back over to the sidewalk, where he stood, gasping for breath. "It's too hot . . . to play tag, Johanna."

He looked up to see Johanna sitting on the sidewalk not ten feet away, crying.

"Johanna," he called, this time softly. He stepped up to her as if she were a bird that would fly away. She looked up, startled to see him.

"*Mein Bruder,*" she said, standing up and wiping away the tears. "My brother. I saw him!"

"Come on, Johanna," said Peter, taking her arm gently. "I don't know what you're talking about."

"Nein!" she insisted. "No! I saw my brother!"

Now she's seeing things, he thought. Then another streetcar rumbled by, and Johanna excitedly pointed at the people sitting in the windows. "In the streetcar," she told him, over and over. "In the STREETCAR!"

"Okay, okay, I get what you're saying. But you can go explain it all to my sister." Peter tried to take her hand, but she refused, not understanding.

"Come on, Johanna. Elise? Talk to Elise? *Sprechen mit Elise?*"

Only when she heard Elise's name did Johanna finally follow Peter. But she looked back over her shoulder at every corner and studied every streetcar that came by. Peter mopped his brow with the short sleeve of his shirt and wished he had an ice cream cone.

"There you are!" said Mrs. Andersen when Peter and Johanna

made it back to the store. "I was wondering . . ."

But as soon as little Johanna saw Elise, she let loose with another torrent of German words.

"She's been trying to tell me something about an imaginary
brother in a streetcar," Peter told his mother. "I guess as soon as
you two went inside the store, she just took off running."

"That's what she's saying," translated Elise. "She says she has
an older brother. Or had."

Peter looked at Johanna, who was still telling her story and
pointing wildly down the street. "But she never mentioned a
brother before."

"I saw him," insisted Johanna. "My big brother Gustav. I saw
him in the streetcar, riding away from me. Now he's gone again."

"Johanna, honey," began Elise, "I'm sure you thought . . ."

Johanna shook her head and looked down at the sidewalk.
"He didn't wave back. I yelled and ran after the trolley. But he
didn't wave back."

Elise got down on her knees and looked the little girl in the
eyes. "Listen, Johanna. I'm sure there are a lot of people who look
like your brother. And it's okay to remember him. But he's not
here, he's . . ."

"How is she going to understand that her brother probably
died in the war?" Peter asked softly.

"It was him," insisted Johanna, setting her jaw and turning
away to look down the street. "I know it was him. I saw him."

Who Holds the Key?

"What time is the awards dinner going to be, again?" asked Peter as his mother got ready to leave.

"Peter, you can never remember times," Elise told him, looking out the window. "Repeat after me: Six o'clock. One hour before seven, one hour after five."

"I was just asking," replied Peter, picking up his pocket Bible out of his suitcase and heading for the door.

"Peter, where are you going?" asked their mother, picking up her purse.

"I just thought I'd go to the lobby and read for a little while."

"That's fine, but did you hear what I said before? I don't want you kids wandering around too far. My hair appointment will only take an hour or so, and then I'll be right back. I want you to stay around here and watch Johanna."

"Sure, Mom," answered Elise.

"This is the last time I'll ask you two kids to do this," continued Mrs. Andersen. "Your father is getting out of his last meeting early, so we'll all have the afternoon together before going to the palace again tonight, okay?"

"I got it, Mom," Peter said with his hand on the doorknob. "I just didn't want to sit around practicing my bows and curtseys with the girls. But we'll stick around until you get back."

Peter was glad to escape to the lobby, where it was quiet for a late Saturday morning. He picked out a big, soft chair not far from the front desk and sank back with his little Bible.

Been a while since I read, Lord, he prayed quietly as he opened the book. *I'm sorry.*

It had actually been weeks and weeks, and Peter couldn't remember the last time. So he just started reading, first a psalm, then skipping over to the New Testament. But between thoughts of the king being hurt and the man from the train, he couldn't focus on the words. He flipped a few pages.

What verse was it that the king read to us? Psalm something . . . Peter tried to remember the conversation as he looked through a few chapters, searching for words that he would recognize.

No, I remember now. Revelation. Last book in the Bible.

Peter turned the pages further until the words seemed to jump out at him.

"These are the words of him who is holy and true," he read quietly, *"who holds the key of David. . . . I know your deeds . . . I know that you have little strength, yet you have kept my word and have not denied my name."*

Peter slammed the Bible shut, almost sorry that he had found what he was looking for. But the words stayed in front of his eyes, and he couldn't shake the feeling that God was trying to tell him something.

"How did you manage to get away from the Germans?" Peter could still hear the voice of the newspaper reporters. *"What did you do?"*

Just luck. Peter opened the Bible back up and stared at the page he had been reading, the part about those who haven't denied His name.

Why didn't I tell everyone how it really happened? he asked himself. *Elise isn't afraid to tell people. Even King Christian came out and said that God was the one who saved Denmark. He didn't say it was just luck. Why don't I ever say the right thing?* His thoughts turned to a prayer. *God, I want to be like the king. I'm tired of being too afraid to say the right thing—*

The sound of the phone ringing jerked Peter out of his quiet prayer. But he kept his eyes buried in his Bible as he listened to the conversation at the front desk.

"No, I'm sorry, he's not in at the moment," said the clerk, Knud-Ole. "Yes, he's still checked in to Room 22. His van is ready? Yes, I'll leave him that message, sir."

Room 22? Peter's ears perked up, and his thoughts quickly shifted to the man from the train. Mr. Eyebrows. *Maybe this time I can see what's going on in his room, since he's not there. Prove that he's up to something.*

Without knowing what he would find, Peter closed his Bible once more and padded quietly up the stairs to the second floor, then down the hallway to the same room where they had been listening through the keyhole.

This time I'm going to find out what's going on here, he decided as he stopped in front of Room 22. *I'm going to find out if it's the last thing I do.*

Peter looked up and down the hallway, then quietly crouched down and pushed aside the "Do Not Disturb" sign to peek through the keyhole below the doorknob. He could barely see the opposite wall, but not much else.

This isn't going to work, he thought, looking back out at the hallway. Still clear. He pulled out the little mirror he had used before to look under a door, then dropped quietly to his knees.

Everything was upside down, but after a moment Peter could make out the inside of the room. It was a lot like their own room, only there was something all over one of the beds. Wires hooked up to small clocks, which were then connected to a cluster of tubes—tubes that looked like huge firecrackers. He had seen something like that before—in a newspaper article on bombs used during the war. Dynamite?

"A bomb!" Peter whispered to no one in particular. His hands began shaking. "That has to be a bomb!"

He pulled his mirror back, stood up, and whirled around to run—but was pinned back to the door by two strong hands belonging to Mr. Tatoo. Beside him stood Eyebrows, his hands on his hips.

"A bomb, you say?" The shorter man seemed amused and furious at the same time, if that was possible. "There must be some mistake."

Peter opened his mouth to yell, but nothing would come out. A moment later he didn't have a choice, as Tattoo expertly clamped his arm around Peter's neck and capped off his mouth with an iron hand. There was no one else in the hallway to see them.

Peter tried to struggle but was, of course, no match for the two men. All he could see was the tattoo of an evil-looking purple snake on the man's arm. Eyebrows unlocked the door, and they dragged Peter into the room.

Peter found his voice by that time, but all he could manage was a muffled groaning sound. He wiggled and squirmed like a puppet whose strings were all tangled. When he tried to kick, Tattoo pushed him to the ground.

"Get something to stuff in this kid's mouth," ordered Eyebrows, this time in German.

Tattoo gave a disgusted grunt and wasted no time finding a towel and some wire. Eyebrows sat on Peter to keep him from getting up. Peter could hardly breathe, and he felt as if his ribs would crack.

"Here," said the wrestler, bringing a towel that looked as if it had been used to polish shoes. Peter felt it pulled into his mouth and tied behind his neck. It even tasted like shoe polish, and tears came to Peter's eyes.

"Ahh-ee!" Peter tried to scream, but it only sounded like a sick goose. "Ahh-ee!"

"Turn on the radio," suggested Eyebrows. Once the loud band music was snapped on, Peter couldn't even hear himself screaming. Then the man roughly yanked Peter's arms in back of him and held them together.

"Now give me that lamp cord," he commanded.

Peter's face was pushed down into the floor, and the man's weight made him gasp for breath. He was obviously heavier than he looked—and much stronger. Peter felt the wire wrapped securely around his wrists, then his ankles. He winced with pain as Eyebrows pulled them up tight.

"Too tight?" asked the man, getting to his feet. Then he laughed, and Tattoo joined in with an odd kind of snorting that might have passed for a chuckle. But at least Peter could breathe, even while his wrists were burning with pain. Eyebrows then tied another cord to hold Peter's wrists close to his feet, stringing them together so Peter could hardly move.

"Do you think he understands German?" asked Eyebrows. He turned Peter over with his boot, leaving Peter to stare helplessly up at the ceiling—and at the two grinning men looking down at him.

"Ah, maybe he picks up a word or two here and there," guessed Tattoo. "I hear Danish kids study a little in school." Then his face twisted to an ugly snarl. "Of course, it doesn't matter if he understands or not. We'll be checked out of here before it makes any difference."

Peter closed his eyes as both men laughed once more.

"That's right, kid," said Eyebrows. "Go ahead and cry. Maybe it will help your pitiful little king."

They laughed again and turned back to their work at the bed, satisfied that Peter could do no harm. And with the radio on, he could make no sound loud enough to attract any attention.

The king! Peter's ears burned to hear what Eyebrows had just said. *What were they talking about? What was this bomb for?* Peter wanted to scream.

"Oh, and by the way," added Eyebrows in his accented Danish. "I sure appreciate your returning my timer to me on the train.

I couldn't have made the bomb without it. Funny how things worked out."

He's no Polish scientist, thought Peter, feeling a strange mixture of pain and anger. He tried to wiggle his hands to keep the circulation going, but his left hand kept falling asleep.

On the bed, the two men worked quickly to connect several more wires to the timer of their bomb. Peter could only watch helplessly from the floor.

"We're running out of time," Eyebrows said finally, glancing down at Peter on the floor. "We have to get to the palace before Eisenhower and all the other VIPs start to get there."

"It would have been a lot easier if we still had von Hanneken's key," grumbled Tattoo.

"Not that key business again." Eyebrows gave the other man a superior look. "That's why we're late, if you ask me. Playing hide-and-seek with those kids. That wasn't the general's plan."

"Well, if General von Hanneken had just given us the key in the first place, instead of hiding—"

"You're not questioning the general, are you, Ludwig?"

"No, no, I hate King Christian as much as he did, it's just that—"

"Well, don't forget he wanted to carry out this plan himself before the war ended. So now it's up to his loyal aides to carry out his last orders. You and me."

Eyebrows stood up and grabbed Tattoo by the shirt collar, unafraid of the much larger man. "So are you with me, or do I have to tie you up on the floor like that boy and do it all myself?"

"No, no, Rolf, I didn't mean that," apologized Tattoo, his hands up. "All I said was I wished we still had the key."

"Listen, would you forget about the stupid key business? I already let you try to get the key. It's just trouble. And I told you ten times we don't need it. That kid at the palace is going to let us in. But if it makes you feel any better, here . . ."

Peter looked up in terror, wondering what the arguing men would do to him. Eyebrows roughly checked into Peter's pockets, pulling out his pocketknife, a couple of marbles, a souvenir ticket from the train ride, and a couple of rubber bands. But no key, of course.

"See?" said the man, throwing Peter's things in a corner. "Now help me finish this thing."

The men turned back to their work.

"You really think the kid at the stable will open up?" Tattoo asked after a few minutes.

"Positive. He thinks we're going to be doing an official security test. And with those Danish police uniforms, nobody is going to stop us." Peter looked over at the other bed, where two sets of black shirts and pants were draped. Eyebrows snorted, amused.

"I'll feel better when I see it happen," Tattoo growled. "I don't like to have to count on anybody for anything. That's why I still wanted the key to the stable door."

The key to the stable door! Now Peter understood. The key he had been carrying all over Copenhagen opened the door to King Christian's stable! And these men, key or no key, were going to put a bomb somewhere in the palace.

"Hitler would have been proud of us—if he were still alive," said Eyebrows, smiling. "Now it's up to us. Nobody stands up to Hitler and gets away with it. Especially not the king of Denmark."

They're crazy, thought Peter, trying not to move.

Eyebrows stripped the end of a wire between his front teeth and attached it to the rear of the clock timer. "All right. I've set it for six-thirty. That gives us plenty of time. They should all be sitting at the banquet table in the main hall by then."

"And then, boom!" Tattoo looked as if he were about to see some fireworks. Then he gave Peter a worried look. "But how about this one? His parents are probably looking all over Copenhagen for him by now. What if they come to the door?"

Eyebrows nodded his head. "You worry too much. But thanks to your wanting the key, they just might. Let's get this stuff cleared off. We're done here."

The two men packed their bomb carefully inside a large gallon can marked with a picture of green peas, the kind of can that a restaurant might use. Peter watched as Tattoo expertly welded the metal bottom back in place. Then he smiled as he lifted it carefully off the table.

"Green peas, anyone?" he chuckled, holding up the can.

"Put that thing away, will you?" ordered Eyebrows.

"Don't worry." Tattoo reached over to place the can into his black leather bag—the same one Eyebrows had been carrying on the train. But his hand slipped and somehow the can squirted out of his fingers.

"Hey!" yelled Eyebrows, covering up his face and ducking.

Peter didn't have time to react. All he could do was stare in horror at the can as it bounced on the hard floor next to the hotel bed and rolled by his head. He closed his eyes, waiting for the explosion.

"I don't know how you survived the war." Eyebrows reached down and picked up the can. "You have got to be one of the clumsiest bomb experts I have ever met. Is that how you lost your finger?"

Tattoo didn't answer, just held open the bag for Eyebrows. Peter noticed for the first time that, sure enough, Tattoo was missing the tip of his little finger on his left hand.

"Sorry," mumbled Tattoo. Eyebrows just grunted and stood up. Then, while Eyebrows peeked out through the window shade, Tattoo put all their spare parts into another bag and stuffed it into a dirty shirt. He walked over to a small steamer trunk by the bed and gave it a kick.

"Think we can fit the kid in here?"

Eyebrows shrugged and looked over at Peter. "I thought that old thing would come in handy. We can probably stuff him in. At least until we can take him to where he won't cause us any more trouble. Maybe somewhere wet."

Peter didn't want to guess what these two men were saying.

He only closed his eyes again and started praying as he hadn't prayed for a long time.

Lord, I don't want to pray to you just for emergencies. I want it to be better than that. But this is an emergency—

Eyebrows and Tattoo picked up Peter like a sack of potatoes and dragged him over to the bed. They rolled him into the trunk and tried to stuff him inside. Peter tried to resist again, but it did no good.

On the radio, Peter could hear one of Elise's favorites, the Andrews Sisters, singing their American harmony. He couldn't understand all the words, but they sounded good to him. *Where is Elise now?* Peter cried with pain as the men closed the top of the trunk over him and roughly forced his head down. The Andrews Sisters sounded far, far away. Then the locks snapped shut, and he was hoisted up into the air, upside down and sideways.

SOMETHING LIKE JONAH

Peter heard a door slam, and then everything was quiet for a moment. He started his moaning sound, but it seemed to make no difference.

"No one's around," said Eyebrows. "It's clear. Here, you carry this side and I'll get the other." Between the two men, Peter felt himself jolted down the hall in his tiny prison.

Funny, thought Peter. *I always thought the idea of hiding in Dad's suitcase and going somewhere sounded pretty exciting. But this isn't quite what I had in mind.*

They stopped for a minute, and Peter thought he heard other voices in the distance.

"We're never going to make it out of here with the kid still awake and making noises," said Tattoo. "What if somebody comes along? We should have—"

"Too late for that now," interrupted Eyebrows. "I think somebody's coming this way. Here, down through this door. We'll take the back stairway to the basement!"

One of the men opened a squeaky door, and then the trunk bounced down three flights of concrete steps. Peter winced every time he hit another bump. Just when he thought the jarring would never end, he jolted to a stop at the bottom of the stairs.

"Now what?" asked Tattoo. "Where are we going to dump the kid so nobody finds him?"

Silence for a minute. Peter thought he heard the voices again in the distance. Voices that sounded a little like Elise. Maybe his mother. But even though Peter screamed as loud as he could, the voices just passed by and were gone again.

"Hey, that's pretty good," said Eyebrows. "No one heard a thing."

"Well, just in case they do, I have an idea."

Peter wondered what more the two Germans could do to him now, and his arms ached from being twisted the wrong direction behind his back. If he were just out of the trunk, he might be able to move his arms around in front. And if he could get some fresh air, that would help, too. . . .

"Here, let's just lift the whole thing up this way," grunted Eyebrows. "No one is going to come down here to the furnace for a long time, at least not during this heat wave. Maybe by November."

Tattoo snorted. "Yeah, November."

Peter felt himself lifted up once more, then balanced on top of something as the men argued.

"Hey, I want this trunk back," complained Tattoo. "What else am I going to use on the trip home?"

Eyebrows sighed. "Yeah, all right. Open the top."

The top of the trunk snapped open, and a moment later Peter was dumped down into a huge pile of sooty coal. He hit the black stuff, which felt something like dusty gravel, rolled, and came to rest on his stomach. The thick dust filled his nose and he began to sneeze. With the gag still in his mouth, Peter could hardly breathe, and he began crying again.

"The kid's getting dust all over me," whined Tattoo.

"Well, I'm terribly sorry about that," replied Eyebrows. "Here, give me a hand with the lid to this thing."

The lid! Peter knew where he had to be, next to the hotel's giant coal furnace. But he didn't know there was a lid to the big bin they had thrown him into. If the two men closed the lid, Peter would have no hope of ever getting free.

"Push it shut, then let's bar the door so they can't just walk down from the lobby. We can get out through the alley door," commanded Eyebrows.

The next sound Peter heard was the slam of a metal top, then the click of a latch. Then everything was quiet except for Peter's raspy crying.

One of the men rapped on the side of the metal coal bin.

"See you later, kid." It was Eyebrows. "Somebody is bound to find you eventually. Have a good summer!"

At least they're gone now, thought Peter as he struggled to turn around. Even though he couldn't sit up, and even though he could hardly breathe for all the coal dust, he felt strangely relieved just to be alone.

But his situation wasn't getting any better. Every time he tried to wiggle around to sit up, the coal crumbled underneath—and he felt as if he was burrowing deeper and deeper into the awful stuff.

He wanted to chew up the towel in his mouth, but it was still too tight. And his arms still ached from being tied behind his back.

Those guys really know how to tie up a person so they can't move.

Peter sat still for a moment and tried to turn his head. But there was nothing to see. It was black inside the coal box. Black in the basement. Black everywhere.

Now I know how Jonah felt, Peter thought. *Only Jonah wasn't all tied up.*

He started to cry again, but that only made him cough until he almost couldn't breathe.

"I'm sorry, God," he groaned. "I've really messed things up."

His prayer reminded him of something, and he stopped crying with a gasp. *My Bible. What happened to my Bible?*

He tried desperately to remember where he had last been holding his pocket Bible. From the lobby, down the hall . . .

Did I still have it when I was walking down the hall?

He couldn't remember.

Maybe I dropped it in the hall. No, maybe I left it on a table in the lobby. I can't remember. But somebody will find it, I hope.

He held on to the hope, even though it wouldn't point anyone to the basement.

It would sure be nice to have my pocketknife right now, but it's on the floor in their room. Doesn't do me a lot of good there.

Peter wiggled a little more and sank even deeper, as if he were in quicksand. It was getting harder and harder to breathe.

I'm sorry, God, he prayed again. That was all that came out. He couldn't get himself to ask God for anything. Not even to help him get out of the mess he was in.

But what am I sorry for? he asked himself. It didn't take long to figure, because the king's voice came back to him, almost as clearly as if the man were in the coal bin with him.

"How do you explain to people?" He remembered the king's question. *"How do you explain how you made it safely through such fantastic adventures?"*

That's what I'm sorry for, he prayed. *I'm sorry for never telling anybody how you always take care of us.*

The electric cords didn't fly off his wrists and ankles, but Peter felt another kind of weight fly off his shoulders. And even with the towel still stuffed in his mouth, he had a strange feeling—like a smile, only on the inside.

Thanks, Lord, he prayed, not fully knowing why.

After that, Peter lost track of time. He wasn't sure if ten minutes or ten hours went by. But he kept wiggling around in his silent, dark world—just to keep the edge of pain away from where the lamp cord held his wrists and ankles tightly bound.

And even though he sank deeper and deeper into the coal, he

kept trying to turn around right side up.

If only I could sit up, he told himself.

Though he kept struggling, his prayers weren't for himself anymore. All he could think of was the palace. The king and the others. All the people who didn't know about the bomb.

Was it already too late?

He kicked with all his strength, wiggled, squirmed, and fought his way until finally he got himself on his side. More kicking, and he finally found himself sitting up.

But this is almost worse, thought Peter. Now his arms were twisted even more cruelly behind his back, and he ended up sitting on his hands. His head was free and his face wasn't in the coal anymore, but he had to duck to not bump the metal lid that kept him trapped.

Maybe if I push up on this. . . .

The lid didn't move. And his hands were getting squeezed tighter. He had to do something quickly.

In all the wiggling, his knots seemed to slide a bit on his wrists. But he knew that the more he pulled, the more they would bite. Still, there was a little hint of a slip on his left wrist. Just a hint.

Hours seemed to pass, and Peter kept wiggling his wrists in spite of the pain. He knew that if he didn't, he would never get out. The hint of a slip on his left wrist turned into a definite loose feeling, and then he could wiggle his wrist even more.

That's it. Just a little more.

His whole body ached from being twisted around. His arms screamed for freedom. But there was a little bit of fresh air coming in through a crack under the lid of the bin. No light, but a little air.

Peter lifted his face up to the air and jerked with all his strength, trying to pull apart the cord that held his hands and his feet together. He jerked once, then twice, and coal dust filled his lungs again. Peter couldn't see, but he felt as if the coal dust had probably coated his sweaty skin.

One more jerk, and something definitely slipped. Peter thought about the friendly king, standing up to give a speech at his dinner party. He could imagine the party Peter and Elise were invited to, all the people in their fancy gowns, uniforms, and tuxedos. Maybe it was starting already.

After this, that white shirt Mom got me with the tight collar is going to seem great.

He took another deep breath, coughed, then blew out all the air in his lungs. He didn't know why it would work, but he remembered seeing a magician get out of handcuffs once doing something like that.

Got it! The cord holding his wrists and feet together finally slipped and Peter kicked his legs free.

Oh! he thought. *That's better.*

Now only his ankles were still held together, as well as his wrists. And he could reach the knots on his ankles—just barely. Another five minutes, and his legs were completely free.

Next he twisted and turned in the coal, flipping over face first again, until he could finally draw his arms under his legs and hold them out in front.

Almost there! he congratulated himself.

With his wrists out in front, he could pick off the awful gag that had been choking him for all these hours.

"Yech!" Peter sputtered and spit once the towel was pulled off.

"At least it kept the coal dust out of my mouth." Peter was glad to talk to himself after so long. Now he could scream properly again.

"Hey!" he hollered at the top of his lungs. The coal dust made him cough. "HEY! HELP!"

Peter listened but heard nothing. The hotel's cellar was still quiet and cool.

"Well, now I just have to take care of these wrists."

Peter set to work chewing the knots that held his wrists together, but the knots were tighter than he had hoped. Even if he could get at the knots with his hands, he wasn't sure he would be able to untie them.

"Unghh!" Peter growled at the cords. He bit into one right down to the metal wire underneath the thin ropelike covering, then tried to yank it apart. That hurt his teeth, but he thought it was better than just sitting there.

"Come on." Peter yanked once more, then again and again. Bit by bit, he tore the cords apart with his teeth, spitting out strings as he did.

"Yech." Peter shook his head and tried to get the wire out of his mouth. But there was nowhere clean to wipe it, so he continued his attack on the cords.

In a few minutes, one of the knots was loosened enough to pull it completely apart. Then another, and another.

"I'm winning, you little knots," he said as he shredded the last one. He groaned as the wires fell from his wrists at last.

"Thank you," Peter whispered as he rubbed his sore wrists and tried to move his aching muscles. "Thank you."

But Peter wasn't free yet. The metal lid over his head was still securely latched. No matter how hard Peter pushed up, it wouldn't budge. And no matter how loudly he yelled, he heard nothing but his own tired voice echoing back at him. Pounding on the side of the metal bin didn't do anything either—except make his fists sore.

Maybe there's a little latch holding this cover down, he guessed. *What would happen. . . ?*

He couldn't think of anything else to do, so he started rocking back and forth, trying to see if he could tip the bin over. It tipped a bit every time he hit the side, but the coal was too heavy.

"GET—" Peter pounded his fist on the side of the bin.

"ME—" He pounded again.

"OUT OF HERE!"

Peter pummeled his little prison, wishing he could pound a hole through the heavy steel.

Nothing can break through, he thought, coughing once more.

Maybe the Germans were right. Maybe I'm going to be stuck down here until November.

He sat still for a minute, trying to think of what to do next.

"Well, I've gotten this far," he told himself. "Correction. God has gotten me this far. Where do I go from here?"

He tried to shake the lid once more, but still it held fast. Something told him that he was going the wrong direction.

Down? There's just a floor.

But he couldn't get away from the feeling that he should try looking deeper—that he should dig down into the coal he had tried so hard to stay away from.

"Okay," he sighed. "I'll dig."

At first Peter could shove a lot of the coal to one side of the bin with his feet. Then he started to dig with his hands, pulling up hands full of coal and throwing them into the other side of the closet-sized bin. When it started to roll down the hill he had created, he began to claw at the coal like a dog digging for a bone.

"I wish I knew what I was looking for," he said to himself as he clawed more and more coal out of his hole. But as quickly as he clawed it away, more coal rolled in to take its place.

At one point Peter brushed against the bottom of the bin, and he touched the bottom corner. Something felt different, very different.

Instead of solid metal, the corner seemed to give way. Peter pushed harder, and suddenly he put his fist right through the rusty lower edge of the coal bin.

"That's it!" declared Peter. He knew why he had dug down to the bottom!

Excitedly, Peter punched more holes through the rust, ignoring the sharp pieces that could have cut his arm. The softest spots were right next to the cement floor of the basement, where the metal box had rusted and rotted the most.

"Yes, yes, yes!" shouted Peter, pushing through with all his strength. The hole widened until it was almost big enough to slip his shoulders through. Even though Peter couldn't see, he could feel the jagged edges of his growing escape route.

He stopped for a moment, trying to catch his breath. He froze as he heard the door at the top of the stairway rattling. *Eyebrows and Tattoo?* He sat completely still, listening. Then, from far away, he thought he could barely hear two familiar voices.

"Elise!" he shouted with all his strength. "I'm down here, Elise!"

It must not have been enough, somehow. The voices faded once again, and Peter pounded at the hole he had been making in the coal bin.

"Elise, can't you hear me?" he asked, the tears coming again. He remembered how Eyebrows and Tattoo had said they were going to put a bar in front of the door to the basement. *Still, you could have tried a little harder, couldn't you, Elise?*

After a few more minutes he turned around so that he could kick his way through the hole, and he widened it even more. But then it got slower. There was a hole, all right, but it wasn't getting much bigger. And it hurt to keep kicking.

Maybe I can just rest, he told himself, trying to breathe. *Get some more strength*.

"It's locked," Peter heard someone say, this time from a different direction. The door from the street into the basement rattled.

"Johanna, it's locked, and why would Peter be in there, anyway?"

Peter couldn't hear an answer, but he thought he heard Johanna's high voice.

"Hey!" yelled Peter. He leaned down to look out his little hole and tried to yell out once more. "I *am* in here! Elise! Get me out of here!"

For a moment there was silence. Then Peter saw the door fly open to the basement and Elise stumbled in.

"Over here!" yelled Peter.

Johanna tripped in behind Peter's sister and ran over to where Peter was trapped.

"I knew you would be here," she announced proudly as Elise got to her feet and came over to investigate. "I knew you would hide here, just like I did."

"Tell her I'm not hiding, Elise," coughed Peter. "Those two German guys tied me up and locked me in here. And what time is it?"

"Oh, Peter." Elise kneeled next to the coal bin and tried to pull some more of the rusty metal out of the way so he could get out. "Mom and Dad are out with the police trying to find you. We're supposed to be staying here with Knud-Ole at the hotel, waiting for calls."

"Elise, you have to tell me what time it is!" he repeated.

" . . . and Mom and Dad are going out of their minds, trying to figure out what—"

"The time, Elise!" screamed Peter, kicking harder at the hole. It was almost big enough to squeeze his shoulders through. "WHAT TIME IS IT?"

"Five-thirty, Peter, but—"

"Like, five-thirty at night?" Peter gave a mighty kick, shredding the side of his shoe. Finally it looked big enough.

"Of course. But it's not dark yet."

"Five-thirty," he groaned. "That's what I was afraid of." He reached both arms out through the hole. "Here, help pull me through."

"Why did they do this to you?" Elise was still puzzled, but she and Johanna grabbed his wrists and pulled.

"Pull!" Peter urged them as he squirmed his way through. He was followed by a load of coal, and then finally Peter was out. For a moment he lay on the floor, gasping for air.

"You . . . you . . ." Elise struggled for words. When he looked up he could see her face was streaked with tears and her eyes were puffy from crying. He scrambled to his feet. Despite his looks, she threw her arms around him and sobbed.

"Elise!" Peter wanted to cry, too, but all he could think of was the clock, ticking down the seconds until six-thirty. Johanna was right there, too, trying to hold on to both of them.

"Elise." Peter held Elise at arm's length by the shoulders. "There's no time. You have to believe what I'm telling you, but I don't have time to explain everything." Another minute had ticked by.

"Elise, those two guys tied me up and threw me in this coal bin because I saw they had a bomb. They're going to put it in the king's palace right now, and they said it's set to go off at six-thirty. You've got to believe me, Elise, really."

Johanna looked at Peter as if he were an alien. And for the briefest of seconds, he looked down at himself. Every inch of his skin was covered with a thick layer of coal dust, and his clothes looked like they had been worn by a chimney sweep.

Boy, is Mom going to be upset when she sees what a mess I've made of these clothes, he thought.

"Dirty," Johanna told him. "You need a bath, Peter."

Peter almost chuckled. Elise looked straight into Peter's eyes for a moment and nodded.

"Are you okay?" she asked.

Peter nodded. "Yeah, I'm fine. But we've got to warn the king before the whole palace is blown up. We only have less than an hour!"

FIFTY-FIVE MINUTES

First stop was the main desk in the lobby, where Peter met a wide-eyed clerk—but not the one they knew.

"Do you know where the Andersens are?" asked Peter, still breathless.

"The Andersens are out with the police, searching for their boy," replied the man. "And however did you think you could come in here looking like that? Get outside this instant!"

"But I'm Peter. I've been trapped in the basement all day by two guys who were in Room 22!"

Peter could already see that he was going to have a hard time explaining. And how much time did they have? Fifty-five minutes? Less?

"Well . . ." the clerk hesitated.

"Look, I can't explain it all right now. But something terrible is going to happen to King Christian if we don't warn him right now!"

"King Christian?" asked the clerk, as if he had never heard of the man.

"Those guys had me tied up all day," huffed Peter. *Why can't he understand?* "And they have a bomb. I *saw* it. They're going to put it someplace where it will go off while the king, and the American General Eisenhower—all those people—are sitting around having dinner!"

The clerk looked at Peter suspiciously. "And how do you know all this?"

Peter wanted to scream. After hours of being tied up in a coal bin, now he had to explain everything.

"I heard them talking," Peter almost yelled. "Listen, can't you call the palace? I could tell the king. He knows me. We're supposed to be at the banquet."

"Oh, so you *know* King Christian, now, do you?" The man smiled slightly, as if he were playing along in some kind of game. "Why don't I call the police for you? You can just sit down over there—no, wait—why don't you stand right outside. I'll call the police, and you can explain your whole story to them."

"Mister, you don't understand," Elise pleaded. "There's not enough time to explain everything all over to the police. There's only—" She looked up at a clock behind the counter. "There's only about fifty-four minutes left. And where's Knud-Ole? He'll believe us, even if you don't."

The clerk held up his hand and nodded as he picked up the phone. "Hello, police?" he spoke softly into the receiver. "Yes, I'll hold. Oh, I see. There's no one in the office who can take . . . well, perhaps it's a slight misunderstanding, but I have here two children who insist—"

The man nodded as he spoke, then smiled. "Yes, of course I'll hold."

Peter raised a cloud of coal dust as he jumped up and down, while Johanna ran her finger curiously across his arm to see what the black stuff was like. Finally he could stand still no more, and started for the door.

The clerk frowned. "Wait a minute. I'm getting through to the police." There was a pause. "Well, I thought I was. No one seems to be answering now."

"Why didn't you tell them it was an emergency?" asked Elise. "Maybe you should call the royal palace."

The clerk fumbled with the dial, slipped with his finger, then tried again. An elderly couple with suitcases backed up a couple of steps from the front desk.

"Please connect me with Amalienborg Palace," the clerk finally croaked into the phone. "This is an . . . er, well, it seems to be somewhat pressing."

Peter looked up at the clock as still another minute ticked by. Five-forty.

"Pressing?" murmured Elise.

"Yes, I'll wait," replied the clerk.

"Tell them you can't!" protested Peter.

The man just shrugged and raised his eyebrows in apology. He said nothing for another moment and just listened to the phone.

"What's wrong?" asked Elise.

"No one answers now," said the man. "It's just ringing and ringing."

Peter hit his forehead. "Fifty minutes!" he groaned. "We have fifty minutes!"

Elise paced around nervously, then faced Peter. "Peter, we just have to—"

"Right." He knew what she was going to say. "But how are we going to get there on time? Do you have any money for a taxi?"

The man behind the counter fished into his pocket for a ten-crown bill. "Here, kids. Now, I have several guests waiting. . . ."

Elise smiled at the man and took the bill. "Thanks," she told him, taking Johanna by the hand. As always, Johanna clutched her stuffed bear tightly. Peter was already on his way out the door.

"Keep trying to phone the palace," Elise instructed the man. "If they don't answer, call the police. Call the army. But call somebody!"

The clerk nodded quickly, and Peter stopped short.

"Oh, one other thing," he added. "Those guys in Room 22—they're not around, are they?"

The clerk shook his head. "The gentleman in 22 checked out several hours ago."

"Thought so." Peter ran out the front door.

"Hey!" yelled Elise, waving down a taxi. Peter saw the big black car with the lighted sign on its roof, too.

Maybe we'll make it in time, after all, he thought as the taxi slowed down.

The car almost stopped, but when the driver caught sight of Peter, he changed his mind and sped on by.

"What?" yelled Elise, waving her arm. "Hey, wait a minute!"

But it was no use. The taxi disappeared in a cloud of blue smoke.

"Now what?" moaned Peter.

They looked left and right, but there was no other taxi in sight. Dozens of people on bicycles were still on the street enjoying the warm evening. And a little white delivery truck with the words "I. Hansen, Plumber" painted on the side had just pulled up to the building next to the hotel. Other than that, the street was quiet.

"Where are we going now, Elise?" asked Johanna. "I thought we already found Peter."

Elise didn't look down. "I'll explain later, Johanna."

Then Elise waved for her brother to follow. "Come on, Peter," she told him. "I have an idea."

Elise ran over to the little truck, where a man in dirty overalls was sitting in the driver's seat, looking over a clipboard. The two front doors hung open.

"Excuse me, sir," said Elise, jumping into the passenger seat. She pulled Johanna up beside her onto a torn green bench seat. Peter followed, a couple of steps behind.

"What?" The man jerked his head up, as if the twins had caught him napping.

"Sir, you're never going to believe this, but there's a life-and-death emergency, and we have to get to the Amalienborg Palace in less than forty-five minutes or the king is going to get hurt."

"Say, haven't I seen you two somewhere before?" The man looked as if he wanted to chat. "Yeah, now I remember. In the paper. You two are the kids who got kidnapped in the German U-boat. That's it. You're the heroes!"

Elise nodded. "That's us. But please, this is an emergency. The palace."

Peter squeezed in next to his sister and held on. Johanna sat on Elise's lap, with the bear on her own lap.

"Well, if you say so," said the man, hesitating only a moment before starting up his truck with a roar. Peter tried to close the door as the truck jerked into gear, but it wouldn't latch tightly.

"Somebody's going to blow up the palace unless we get there first," Elise told their driver.

"WHAT?" The man panicked as the van shot out into traffic. "Why didn't you say so in the first place? Is it those Nazis again?"

"German guys." Peter shouted back over the roar of the engine. "They used to work for the German General von—whatever his name was . . ."

"Von Hanneken," added Elise.

"Yeah, von Hanneken," Peter said. "The one who had some kind of plan to hurt the king before the war was over."

The plumber's expression clouded. "And they want to carry out the general's last command, do they? Well, no one's going to hurt King Christian as long as Ib Hansen has anything to say about it!"

The man's beefy hands gripped hard at his steering wheel. They rocketed around a corner, jolting off the curb. A pile of pipes and tools came loose in the back of the covered delivery truck.

"Don't worry about that," he told them. "How much time do we have?"

Elise checked her watch. "Twenty-five minutes."

They were almost there, and they hadn't stopped for a single stop sign.

"Lunatic!" yelled a man on the sidewalk who dropped his bag of groceries as they screeched by him. "Get off the sidewalk!" Potatoes rolled in every direction.

Peter closed his eyes and tried to hang on to the door handle, afraid the loose door might fly open any second. As they screamed around another curve, the door popped open and he slid off the end of his seat, still hanging on to the door handle.

"Out of the way!" their driver shouted and waved at a herd of bicyclists, scattering them in every direction. He didn't notice that Peter was suspended over the street, stretched like a hammock between the open door and the seat of the truck.

"Peter!" called Elise. Her brother was afraid to look down, afraid to let go of the open door. They missed a terrified woman on a bicycle by what seemed like less than an inch.

"Excuse me," whispered Peter, dangling over the sidewalk. Elise grabbed him by the belt and yanked him back to safety.

"You'd better ride in here," she told him.

Peter nodded and slammed the door, hard. "Thanks, Elise."

But their driver acted as if he hadn't noticed. A minute later he gave Peter a curious look. "That door doesn't always close very good. Say, what happened to you anyway? Been playing in a chimney?"

"It's a long story," replied Peter. He looked ahead of them as the truck weaved in and out of traffic. "We're almost there?"

In a moment the familiar palace square was in sight.

"Okay, tell me where you want to stop," said Ib Hansen as they streaked into the square.

"Main palace," pointed Peter. "Over there."

"Front door," agreed Elise. "Twenty-three minutes."

Mr. Hansen brought his van to a screeching stop and they piled out after Peter wrenched open his door. But two of the king's black-hatted guards stood ready with their rifles drawn.

"You're not going in there," one of the guards told them, stone faced.

"We're Peter and Elise Andersen," began Elise, "and there's a bo—"

"I don't care if you're the queen of Spain," interrupted the guard impatiently. "You have to have an invitation to get in there. Do you have an invitation?"

"We do," replied Elise, "but it's back in the hotel room. But, listen, this is an emergency."

"Right," replied the guard. "Maybe you can go home and get it for me after you take a hot bath."

"You don't understand," protested Peter. "We have to get in there to warn the king!"

For a few seconds there was total confusion as Peter and Elise tried to explain what was going on. Johanna looked as if she was going to start crying.

The plumber strutted over to help, pulling on his grease-stained overalls as he walked. "Listen, pal, don't you know who these kids are?"

The guard didn't loosen his grip on his rifle. "My orders are not to let anyone else in after all the guests have arrived." He gave Peter a withering stare. "But if you insist, I'll have someone go and check on what you're saying."

Peter stared helplessly as another guard was called.

We don't have time for this! he thought, jamming his hands into his pockets. *Maybe I can run for the door.* His pockets were full of coal dust, but then he remembered what had started all his problems.

The key! How could he have forgotten?

Without wasting another precious second arguing with the guards, Peter backed away from the group, grabbed Johanna's hand, and disappeared around the back of the plumber's truck. Ib Hansen was still arguing with one of the guards. Once Peter was sure no one was looking, they slipped over to the stable door.

"Shh," Peter told the little German girl. She looked back to where Elise was standing.

"Where are we going, Peter?" she asked.

"Time for Alfred the bear to give me back the key," he told her, trying to remember again the words to say in her own language. She looked as if she didn't quite understand.

"Schlüssel, remember, Johanna?" he told her. "The key?"

Johanna smiled and pointed to her bear's stomach. "Oh, the key. Alfred still has it in his tummy."

"Great, because I need it back now," Peter tried to explain as best he could. "Ich NEED IT."

This is going to be the hard part, thought Peter. He looked around and wondered how loudly Johanna would scream if he tried to tear open the stuffed animal to get his key.

"Can I see Alfred?" he asked.

Johanna looked suspiciously up at Peter but handed the bear over.

"You're not going to hurt him, are you?" she asked.

"No, no. Just for a minute."

Peter could feel the big metal key behind where Elise had sewn it in place. Then he saw what he was looking for—a loose thread!

"Look, Johanna, I know how much you like this bear. But we can fix him."

Johanna didn't understand. But as Peter tried to explain to her, he unraveled the loose thread and pulled back a corner of the fur. There was the key! With a yank he had it in his hand, as well as a bit of stuffing.

"Hey!" said Johanna, taking back Alfred.

"It's okay," Peter assured her. "Elise can fix it again."

Johanna held the bear tightly as Peter fumbled with the key.

It has to fit, he told himself, trying the key in a large keyhole. The lock was sticky and stubborn, but the key went in with a gritty complaint. Peter pushed as hard as he could, then pulled. One of the big double doors swung open.

Inside, Peter stared for a moment at a dark blue delivery van parked just inside the gate.

Odd place to park, he thought as he slipped into the stable and slammed the door behind him. Johanna was like a shadow. He ran inside and searched the straw-covered floor by the secret door.

Or, at least, where he thought the secret door was. One of the horses stomped nervously in the stall next to him as he pushed saddles and bridles out of the way.

"Where is that thing?" he grumbled.

"Did you lose something, Peter?" asked Johanna, as sweetly as if he had just dropped something on the floor at home.

"I'm looking for a door," he told her again, then paused for a second to explain in German. "*Eine Tür.* That's what I'm looking for. Eine Tür. A door."

"Oh, I see," said Johanna, dropping to her knees. She held her bear out in front of her, as if it were looking for the door, too, in some kind of grand game. She made the bear dig around in the straw just as Peter had been doing. A second later she began tugging on something.

"Alfred found the door, Peter. Is this it?"

Peter reached over and clapped her on the back. "You found it, Johanna! Or Alfred. Whatever. Good job." He pulled at the small handle to the trapdoor. "Now listen, I want you and Alfred to go back out and find Elise, okay? I have to do something here. Please—go get Elise!"

Peter pointed back out at the street, and stepped down into the hole—just as the big door to the street swung open. Johanna looked uncertainly back at Peter, then obediently ran for the street door.

"Oh no," Peter whispered to himself as he ducked down the stairway. "The guard?"

There has to be enough time! thought Peter as he stumbled down the stairway to the tunnel's main level. Even without a watch, he knew he had only a few short minutes before the bomb was set to go off. Maybe seconds.

No one followed him, though he heard the noise of someone running across the wooden stable floor above his head. Once Peter was in the main section of the tunnel, he raced as fast as he could through the darkness, waving his arms wildly out in front. Twice he bounced off the wall, but he just picked himself up and kept running.

"Peter!" A voice echoed through the tunnel from somewhere behind him. It sounded almost as if Elise were standing right next to him. "Are you in there?"

"Over here, Elise," Peter shouted back. "I'm almost to the end. Don't come in here."

"We're coming after you!"

"I can't wait, Elise."

Peter crashed on, trying to remember the twists and turns of the short tunnel. As he hurried around what he thought was the last turn, he lost his balance on a patch of gravel and fell on his back.

"Peter?" called Elise, her voice echoing through the tunnel.

Peter, stunned for just a moment, couldn't answer. But a second later Elise and Johanna tripped over him and tumbled to the ground in a tangle of elbows, arms, and legs.

"Peter, that better be you, Peter . . ."

"It's me," Peter finally managed to whisper. He got to his knees and held his hand out in the darkness. All he could feel was Alfred.

"What are you doing down there on the floor?" asked Elise, picking herself up.

"Slipped." Peter reached out and felt Elise's shoulder, then gave it a tug. "Come on!"

They were almost to the king's closet when they hit the inside wall. Peter groped around for a handle, but again it was hard to find. This time he just kicked at the door with all his strength, breaking one of the hinges and sending the door clattering to the floor inside the palace. Peter half crawled, half stumbled into the royal library.

Almost there, he thought, slipping in on the polished marble floor.

The next few seconds went by as if they were in slow motion. Peter and Elise made it out to the hallway, with Johanna right behind them. Someone in the palace staff immediately shouted a warning.

"Hey!" yelled a maid, carrying an armload of tablecloths. "What are you kids doing here?"

Peter sprinted down the building's main hall and up a short flight of stairs toward the banquet room. But in front of the door stood two large men, talking to each other. They turned to face Peter when they heard the maid's shout.

Peter couldn't slow down; Elise and Johanna were right on his heels. They slipped down the hallway and the men stepped up to hold them back. Peter had never played baseball, but he made a perfect slide under the men's arms and directly into the double doors to the ballroom. One of them grabbed Peter's sleeve and ripped his shirt just as Peter yanked open the doors and stumbled into the grand ballroom.

"There's a bomb in here!" screamed Peter as loudly as he could manage. "It's going to go off, like right now!"

For a moment the man loosed his grip on Peter's shirt, and Peter popped to his feet. There was a murmur of shock from everyone in the room. Peter looked up to see a long table, festively decorated with flowers and flags, and important-looking people all dressed up in their fanciest clothes, sitting in long rows. The king and queen were placed in the middle of the long table. At the king's side, Peter recognized the American General Eisenhower, a balding man with a smile frozen on his face.

"King Christian, you've got to get out!" Peter yelled as he got to his feet. "You've got to believe me. There's a bomb in here somewhere, set to go off at six-thirty!"

Everyone looked to the king, and several more men made a

move to grab Peter. Dishes crashed to the floor, and one of the women screamed. General Eisenhower stood up, and a man in a brown American army uniform rushed to his side. But King Christian put up his hand.

"Do what he says," commanded the king. "General Eisenhower, I apologize. Everyone must now get out of the room."

The king's face looked serious, and the crowd of about one hundred people made a move for the door. The American general was surrounded by three soldiers. Queen Alexandrine, dressed in a brilliant blue formal dress, helped the king to his feet.

Peter turned to his sister. "They're not going to get out of here in time."

Think, Peter, he commanded his terrified brain. *Where is that thing? The bomb in the can of peas. . . .*

He looked around to see a side entrance where several people were trying to get out through a pair of swinging doors.

"Elise!" Peter shouted at his sister. "Maybe it's in there. That kitchen!"

Without another thought Peter vaulted over a table and through the double doors. In the kitchen, three wide-eyed women in white aprons looked at Peter. One of them dropped her mixing spoon.

"Peter, over there." Elise grabbed Peter's arm and pointed across the kitchen at a serving cart piled high with supplies. Along with sacks of sugar and flour, the cart held several cans, just like the one the bomb was hidden inside. And for a moment, Peter froze.

"Two minutes, Peter. Maybe three."

Gritting his teeth, Peter slipped over to the cart and looked for the right can. Then he looked up at his sister in desperation.

"They're all alike. I can't tell!" he yelled as he wheeled the cart through the kitchen and past the terrified cooks. Elise cleared the way. They burst through the double doors and into the great dining hall, where several people were still milling around, confused. Peter's target was one of the large floor-to-ceiling windows lining the grand hall.

No time to open the window, he thought. *Hope they don't mind!*

With all his strength Peter rammed the cart straight through the window, pushing it through a cascade of shattering glass. At the last minute he let go and watched the cart tumble through the air before it crashed into a flower bed in the yard behind the palace.

"What's going on up there?" yelled a guard from down below, running toward the mess in the garden.

Peter shook his head in horror, then both he and Elise waved furiously.

"Get away!" yelled Elise. "Get back!"

"There's a bomb down there about to explode!" shouted Peter.

But the guard didn't seem to hear as he trotted toward the cart.

"What did you say?" the guard yelled back, picking up the broken wooden pieces of the cart from out of the mangled flowers. He looked annoyed.

"The can of peas!" screamed Elise. "It's a bomb!"

Even from the second floor Peter could see the young man's eyes grow as big as baseballs as he finally understood. As if a snake had bitten him he threw the can in the flower bed and started running wildly in the opposite direction.

Peter pulled back from the window, closed his eyes, and covered his face with his arm. But all he heard was the guard's footsteps running across the small backyard behind the palace.

Seconds ticked by. No explosion. Peter opened one eye, then the other. Elise was peeking out the window.

"Get away from the window, Elise," Peter warned her, just as a muffled explosion rattled the side of the building. Someone screamed.

A tall man in a military uniform leaned out the broken window to inspect the damage as a puff of sharp smoke drifted up to the second story.

"Not much of a bomb," he reported. "I've seen Chinese fire-crackers more powerful."

Puzzled, Peter leaned out the window with the rest of them. "Why would they have done that?" he wondered. The bushes were torn up around the toppled cart, but there was more of a mess from the broken window and the scattered flour and sugar.

"Is this some kind of sick joke?" asked a man behind them. Peter was afraid to turn around.

The crowd of people began to buzz with questions, and a tall man in a dark tuxedo grabbed Peter and Elise by the arms. "You have some explaining to do, kids," he told them gruffly.

Peter's head was still swimming. "No, wait a minute," he protested. "There were two Nazi guys. I can explain—"

Suddenly the buzzing in the ballroom stopped as everyone noticed Susanne, the king's assistant, being led into the room. Her face was pale, and she seemed to be limping as she hung on to a man's arm for balance. She looked up with desperation in her eyes.

"Someone's taken King Christian!" she croaked. "They jumped on us in the hallway and hit me."

"What?" asked someone in amazement.

Susanne took another breath. "I'm okay. But someone's taken King Christian!"

Follow the Trail

Once again, the palace seemed to explode with confusion. Guards ran everywhere, checking entries and exits. The tall man in the tuxedo let go of Peter and Elise to follow one of the guards to the front of the palace.

"Check all the exits!" he shouted to no one in particular. And suddenly it all made sense to Peter. He remembered the phone call back at the hotel, when he had been reading his Bible. The one about a van.

"Elise, the tunnel," he told his sister, taking her hand. "There was a blue van parked in the stable. I should have known it was the getaway car. Now they have the king, and they have a head start."

Elise nodded seriously as they slipped through the crowd, ran down the stairs, and headed for the room with the entrance to the tunnel.

"I hope Johanna's okay," she said as they opened the door.

A moment later the twins were crouched in the tunnel once more, trying to see ahead of them.

"I'm sure she's fine. Can you find the light?"

"It's still out," said Elise, flipping the switch on and off.

"Doesn't matter," replied Peter, taking a step. "We can find the way."

But two steps into the darkness, Peter almost tripped over something. He held out his hands to stop his fall.

"It's the king's wheelchair!" he told Elise, not stopping. "They left it here. I knew they would."

"So you think the whole thing about the bomb was just a fake?"

"I don't know, Elise."

Peter pushed on through the tunnel, moving as fast as he could.

"I'm still worried about Johanna," replied Elise. "She's probably scared to death somewhere in the palace."

"I'm sure she's fine. Mom and Dad might even be there by now."

"So where are we going? Maybe we should wait."

"Elise, there's no time for that. The king is in danger. Nobody will believe us, just like before. We would have to explain it all to them. And by the time we could find somebody who would believe us about what happened to King Christian, those German guys would be out of the country. Here, help me get the door."

A moment later Peter and Elise both stood blinking for a moment in the light of the stable. But instead of horses and hay it smelled like a cloud of exhaust smoke.

"Now what?" asked Elise. "We missed them. And we don't even know which way to go."

"Well, the delivery van just left. All we have to do is find it."

Peter started to push open the door to the street, but stopped when he heard a groaning noise from somewhere back in the stable. "Did you hear that?" he asked his sister.

"I heard it," she replied, running back to investigate.

It wasn't hard to find where the noise came from. Jens, the stableboy, was sitting in the corner of one of the horse stalls, wrapped up in a pair of leather reins used to guide horses. His mouth was tied securely with a rag, just like Peter's had been when he was dumped into the coal bin.

"Oh!" he sighed, as Peter and Elise untied him. "Am I glad you're here! King Christian! Those men have taken the king!"

"We know that," replied Peter, helping Jens to his feet. "But which way? How did they get in here?"

The stableboy rubbed his wrists as he ran to the door. "They told me they were doing a security test, making sure that the tunnel was secure." He stopped for a second and threw down the leather strap in anger. "And I thought they were for real. It's all my fault."

"There's no time for that now," said Peter. "We've got to find the king!"

"And Johanna," added Elise.

"Did they say anything about which way they were going?" Peter asked Jens. "Anything at all?"

Jens shook his head. "They were laughing, saying something about how their plan worked, and about dumb kids."

"That's us." Peter hit the wall with his fist.

From outside in the palace square, they could already hear sirens and shouting. And before they could open the door to the street, Johanna burst through.

"Elise!" she cried, bursting into tears.

"There you are!" Elise wrapped her arms around the frightened little girl. "I was worried to death about you. Where have you been?"

Johanna did her best to talk through the sobs. "I was scared. All the people were running and shouting. I thought maybe airplanes were coming again."

"Airplanes? What airplanes?" Peter looked puzzled.

Elise nudged her brother. "You know, Peter. The bombers. The war. Remember where she's from."

Peter nodded. "Right."

"I couldn't find you or Elise," Johanna continued, catching her breath. "So we followed the king."

"We?" Peter wrinkled his forehead. "What does she mean, 'we'?"

Elise closed her eyes for a second. "Her and the bear, Peter."

I should have known, Peter told himself.

"Did they see you?" asked Elise.

Johanna shook her head. "I was quiet. They didn't stop. And they were mean. I saw they pushed that boy when he tried to stop them." She pointed at Jens.

"So where did they go after that?" asked Peter impatiently. "Which way?"

Johanna took his hand and pulled him out the door. Black police cars were screaming into the square, sirens wailing. Johanna pointed left, down Frederik's Street, toward the big green copper dome of Frederik's Church. The few stores that had been open Saturday afternoon were closed by that time, but curious people were starting to come out of their apartments, staring their direction.

"That way," she told them.

"Then where?" Peter asked again.

Johanna started to cry once more.

"Come on, Johanna," he insisted. "We have to know!"

Johanna looked up the street, then pointed to the left.

"Good, Johanna, good. Now, did they say anything that you heard?"

Johanna buried her face in Elise's shirt and sobbed. "Boat," she choked out between sobs.

"Boat?" pressed Peter. "Are they going to a boat?"

Johanna's shoulders shook with her crying. But she nodded.

Peter looked at his sister. "We need some help."

"But, Peter, they'll never believe us," she answered, holding Johanna tightly. "Not after what happened with the bomb, or whatever it was."

Peter pulled his hair, panicking. Then a guard by the main palace entrance across the square sighted them.

"You kids!" he shouted, pointing his finger at them. "What are you doing over there?"

"Oh no," moaned Peter. "We're in trouble again."

"Open the door wider," yelled Jens from behind them. They looked around to see the young stableboy sitting on top of the king's horse, Jubilee, bareback. "It was my fault those guys got in. I'm going to go find the king!"

"On that?" asked Peter, not waiting for an answer. The guard was running across the square.

"I'm going, too," decided Peter.

Jens hesitated only a second. He saw the guard, leaned over, and hoisted Peter up behind him.

"I'll get them to help us," promised Elise. "They'll listen."

"Stop!" ordered the guard. But he was still too far away.

"Sorry!" Peter yelled back.

Peter squeezed his legs around the big black horse's back as tightly as he could and grabbed Jens around the waist, while Jens brought the sturdy horse to a fast trot.

"Hold on!" cried Jens. They turned down Frederik's Street and around the Saturday night traffic. In a moment, they faced the big Frederik's Church, then wheeled left again and straight through the intersection. Peter closed his eyes and held his breath as a car blared its horn.

"Hey, what do you think you're doing?" someone yelled at them.

Jubilee seemed to sense their emergency and quickened his pace as Jens made a loud kissing sound with his lips.

"Come on, Jubilee," Jens urged the horse.

Any faster, and I'm going to fall off, thought Peter, bouncing hard on the horse's back. He gritted his teeth and kept his eyes shut.

The traffic in that part of town began to thicken, with trucks crowding them into the center of the avenue that led down to the Royal Theater.

"Hey, I think I see the van," said Jens, pointing off ahead of them, through the traffic. Peter opened his eyes.

"I don't know. Are you sure?"

"No, but what else do we have to go on?"

Peter looked ahead once more, squinting his eyes. It looked like the wrong color—black instead of blue. But maybe . . .

Next to them a car honked its horn. Frightened, Jubilee pulled up for a moment. The next thing Peter knew, he was sliding off the side of Jubilee's back, clutching at air.

"Whoa!" yelled Peter, falling hard to the pavement. A couple of motorbikes raced past, and the horse bolted on.

By the time Jens was able to rein in Jubilee, he was already almost a half-block away. Peter got to his feet, wondering if he had broken anything. For once, he seemed to have bounced.

Jens looked over his shoulder, but Peter waved him on.

"Go!" shouted Peter, cupping his hands around his mouth like a megaphone. "Keep going. I'll catch up."

With a nod Jens pulled the horse back into traffic and galloped on toward the van they had seen. Peter stood in the middle of the avenue, watching the traffic go by in both directions. Hot tears of frustration filled his eyes, then he jumped when someone on a motorbike honked his little horn at him. He could hear sirens in the distance.

"I can't give up now," he said out loud. He trotted back to the sidewalk and kept running.

Up ahead, a group of boy scouts in dark green shirts and shorts were marching his way, two by two, taking almost the entire sidewalk. A drummer was in the lead of the troop parade. Peter ran up to the group.

"Hey, kid," shouted one of the boys. "Want to go on a campout? We're going tomorrow morning. Maybe if you take a bath first, though . . ."

Peter shook his head, trying to catch his breath. But the boy scout parade didn't stop, and Peter had to walk backward to keep up with them. The scoutmaster, a young man in the same color uniform, marched in the rear.

"Uh-uh," said Peter. "Not this weekend. But maybe you can

help me. I'm looking for a van, like a blue van? Did you see one coming down the street from the palace?"

"Hey, Torben," piped up one of the boys toward the back. "Tell him about the guy on the horse."

A freckle-faced older boy marching next to the drummer looked curiously at Peter. He put out his hand for the drummer to stop. "There was a van that almost ran us over a couple of blocks back." Then he turned to another one of the scouts, a boy about Peter's age. "Which way did he go, Lars?"

"Turned off toward Nyhavn—New Harbor," replied the boy, jerking his thumb in the direction of the crowded waterfront area famous for sailors' boardinghouses, bars, and loud music. "But what are you, some kind of chimney sweep?"

Some of the boys chuckled, and Peter took a deep breath. "Listen, you have to believe me. This is life and death. Hear that siren?" he asked. A number of the scouts turned their heads. "Two guys in that blue van have kidnapped King Christian!"

The boys broke their lines and gathered around Peter, trying to find out more. But he just shook his head and held up his hands. "There's not enough time. We just have to go find him!"

The twenty-five boys looked at their two leaders: a man in his early twenties, and the oldest boy, Torben.

"What do you think, Mr. Lind?" asked Torben. "Sound like a joke to you?"

The scoutmaster studied Peter's face for a moment. "To Nyhavn!" ordered the man. "Stay in your ranks, double-time!"

The boys cheered and got back in line, while the drummer started up again. Peter ran along beside the two rows of uniformed boys, jogging as fast as he could. A couple of minutes later Peter heard a horse's hooves clip-clopping behind him.

"Hey!" yelled Jens. "I followed the wrong van. Where are you going?"

"Nyhavn!" Peter yelled over his shoulder. "The scouts saw them turn that direction."

Nyhavn was one more block down the avenue and then two

blocks toward the bay. Not far, but Peter was sweating by the time they got closer to the old waterfront neighborhood.

"Look for the blue van," ordered the older scout.

And then what do we do? wondered Peter.

"There it is!" shouted one of the scouts. Before Peter could say anything, they all broke away from their line and sprinted for a light blue van.

"Wait!" he tried to warn them. "That's not the one."

But it was too late. The boys swarmed over the van, knocking on the sides and opening up the doors.

"That's not the one!" repeated Torben, trying to get their attention. "Dark blue. The real van is dark blue."

One by one the scouts peeled themselves away from the light blue van, leaving a shaken driver staring out at them. Wide-eyed, the man shook his head and rolled up his window.

"Sorry, sir." Torben tried to apologize, but the van started up and left them in a cloud of smoke. The scout leader shrugged and looked up ahead.

"Three more blocks and we run into the bay," he observed as they ran down the narrow waterfront street. "They have to be here somewhere."

Peter nodded and tried to keep up. The kidnappers could have crossed the Holberg drawbridge that spanned the narrow dead-end canal. They could have gone anywhere in the city, maybe parked and ran. But there were so many old five-story buildings along this stretch of the harbor. So many hiding places.

"Straight?" asked one of the scouts. "Or right, over the bridge?"

For a moment they all stopped, next to the bridge. Peter looked straight to where the canal opened out into Copenhagen's bay. The van could still be parked somewhere along the crowded waterfront. Or across the bridge? They could be over there, too.

"I know," said Torben. "We'll split up and keep going along both sides."

Just then something caught Peter's eye at the far end of the

Nyhavn canal. A boat going faster than it should have been in the narrow waterway.

"Wait a minute." Peter pointed down the canal. "What's that?"

"Is that your man?" asked the scoutmaster.

Peter shook his head. "Too far away. Can't tell. But maybe . . ."

Jens pulled up on his horse and stopped to look as well.

"I think that's him," said the stableboy. "Someone just ducked down behind the steering wheel."

The boat was getting close, throwing up spray on either side. It was a polished wooden express cruiser, long, sleek—and fast. Someone stooped behind a windshield in the middle of the boat, studying them as it got closer to the bridge. The boat was low enough to slip underneath without anyone having to open the drawbridge.

"That's one of them!" cried Peter. Even from a distance he could make out the tall figure of the wrestler, Tattoo. His police uniform shirt was torn and open in front. "We've got to stop him!"

As the boys crowded up onto the bridge, Peter saw a little white English convertible keeping pace with the motorboat from the opposite side of the canal. The little two-seater reminded Peter of the racecar playing piece for a Monopoly game. But someone inside it was pointing at them. Tattoo glanced to the side and increased his speed.

"Hey, look back there!" shouted one of the scouts, looking down at the water from the bay side of the bridge. A long, wide, open tour boat was just passing underneath.

"And now, as we pass into the New Harbor area," Peter heard the tour guide reciting his speech, "you'll see the houses on the right, where Hans Christian Andersen once rented an apartment. The famous writer was . . ."

On a collision course, the cruiser was picking up more speed as it raced toward them on the bridge. Too fast to stop. There was only one thing to do.

"Into the tour boat!" yelled Peter. He stepped over the railing on the bay side of the bridge and hopped straight down, almost stepping straight into the half-empty seats of the boat as it scraped under the low bridge. A dozen boys in the scout troop acted fast enough to follow him, dropping like ripe fruit from a tree.

An older woman gasped as they tumbled over the seats. But Peter and his troop got to their feet and ran to the controls.

"See here," complained the tour guide. "What's the meaning of this? I'm calling the police."

"I wish you would," said Peter, trying to think of a way to sound polite under the circumstances. "But the king . . . we have to block that boat!"

When the tour-boat man hesitated, Torben slipped in behind Peter, grabbed the steering wheel, and turned it hard.

"Sorry," said Torben, repeating what Peter had said to him a few minutes before. "This is life or death. King Christian's in that boat."

"The king?" echoed the tour-boat man, suddenly letting go of the wheel. "Why didn't you say so?"

For a sickening moment it looked as if the cruiser with the wild-eyed Tattoo at the steering wheel would slice the heavy, bargelike tour boat in half. But then Tattoo swerved hard to the right just as their tour boat swung broadside like a door to the canal. It stretched from one side of the canal to the other, nearly as long as the bridge.

Only a small gap remained at the far end, behind them, and Tattoo was steering for the gap. He slowed down for an instant, grinding along the wooden posts on the side of the canal like a bumper car in a carnival, scratching along the back end of the tour boat.

"He's getting through!" yelled Torben, jumping to the rear of the boat, nearest to where Tatoo was slipping through. "Put it in reverse!"

The tour-boat man did throw his boat into reverse, but it was too late. With a moaning and terrible scraping, the beautiful wooden cruiser looked as if it was going to slip through the narrow gap. The cruiser's engines roared with power, throwing up a fountain of foam behind the boat. Something splintered as the two boats met, while Tattoo reached over and quickly latched the door to the forward compartment, right next to where he stood steering.

Peter ran to the back of the tour boat with the others, where Tattoo looked like a trapped wild animal. The German would be free in just a moment, unless . . .

"Tackle him for King Christian!" ordered the scout leader, launching himself off the end of the boat and straight into Tatoo. Two of the older scouts followed with Peter.

"You! But how?" Tattoo snarled in German, just as his boat shot full speed under the bridge and down the canal. He tried to steer down the middle while swinging at his unwelcome guests.

All four boys fell upon Tattoo at once, tearing him away from the controls of the boat. But he wasn't going to give up that easily. One of his frenzied swings glanced off Peter's face, catching him right by the eye. But despite his strength, Tattoo was hopelessly outnumbered. He growled like an injured grizzly bear and pulled them all around the open back end of the cruiser.

Peter buried his head in the man's stomach, hoping to hold on hard enough to keep him still. Instead, he felt himself pulled around with the rest of the group, carousel-style. In a single bunch they tumbled over the short back railing of the boat and into the water.

Peter did a somersault, and with his open mouth he felt as if he was gargling salt water.

But by the time he looked up, he could see black police cars racing along both sides of the canal with their lights flashing. The white English convertible raced in between two of the patrol cars and screeched to a stop near where they had been dumped into the water. Someone jumped out of the passenger side and ran to the water's edge. Peter shook his head above the water and his eyes cleared.

"Peter!" yelled Elise, waving at him wildly with both arms. .

Susanne from the palace was soon next to her, and so was little Johanna. "Over here!"

Peter was more worried to see the express cruiser still moving down the canal, this time without a driver. It slowed down, bumped off one side, then another, then wedged in behind a large fishing cutter with a wood-splitting sound that made Peter wince.

Johanna was fascinated to see such a thing, and stood at the edge of the canal to see better. By that time Tattoo had dog-paddled over to the edge of the canal right below where Johanna was standing, watching the cruiser. Peter saw Tattoo pull himself up the six-foot-tall timbered wall and reach for Johanna's legs.

"Look down, Johanna!" yelled Peter. He wasn't sure if Johanna or his sister understood who was in the water and who was still in the cruiser. Elise looked down, yelped, and leaped forward to grab the little girl just as Tattoo reached for Johanna's ankle.

"Let go of her!" screamed Elise, pulling back on Johanna's shoulders. Tattoo pulled just as hard at Johanna's shoe, and the frightened little girl became the middle of a human tug-of-war.

"If you had just given us the key," the man bellowed in desperation, "none of this would have happened."

"Let me go!" cried Johanna. "You're hurting me."

Elise started to slip, but there was nothing to hold on to. Peter swam their way, about halfway across the canal, but Susanne was quicker. She pulled off her shoe and used it like a club, hitting Tattoo square on the top of the head and knocking him backward off the ledge where he had perched.

Peter reversed direction as Tattoo came splashing back into the canal, while two police cars pulled up on either side of the girls. With so many policemen on hand, Tattoo had little choice but to climb back up to dry land and into the waiting arms of the officers.

By that time the tour boat had pulled up to where the three scouts and Peter were splashing.

"There's one more," Peter panted as the scouts pulled him to safety back into the tour boat. "Two guys. One more in the boat."

He kept his eyes on where the cruiser was now caught tightly, its engines still racing. And by that time the tour-boat operator didn't need anyone to convince him; he had his boat backed around and was heading at full speed to the trapped cruiser. So were several police cars, and the convertible with Elise, Susanne, and Johanna.

"There's another guy inside the boat with the king," Peter shouted to the scoutmaster as they edged closer. "But I think the door is locked from the outside."

Mr. Lind nodded and stood ready on the front edge of the tour boat.

"Careful now, boys," the leader warned them. "I don't want any of you getting hurt."

Peter looked around at the troop and almost had to laugh, even after what they had gone through. They were perched on the edge like a pack of hounds, and the leader was warning them not to get hurt.

"What if he has a gun?" squeaked a voice from behind Peter.

Mr. Lind straightened up for a moment and looked back over his shoulder, as if he had just thought of that possibility for the first time. He looked around at the police cars coming their direction, nodded, and held his hands out to the sides.

"You're right, Lars. Let's let the police take it from here."

That was when the door of the cruiser flew open with a crash and Eyebrows came flying out, fists up. Standing next to the splintered door, he stopped short, as if he couldn't quite decide what to do. For a long second they stared at each other—the fox and the hounds.

"It's the second one!" blurted the scoutmaster.

This time no one hesitated. Twenty boys flooded aboard the cruiser, yelling like a soccer team after a winning goal. They dog-piled on top of Eyebrows before the little man had a chance to move.

"Don't hurt him, boys," commanded the scoutmaster. "Just sit on him for a minute until the police get here."

"Stupid kids!" groaned Eyebrows. Like Tattoo, his fake police uniform was rumpled and unbuttoned. Then he caught sight of Peter and groaned even louder. "I knew we should have dumped you in the bay. You and that king of yours."

"Hey, where *is* the king?" asked Torben.

Peter bypassed the wild dog-pile, stepping over two boy scouts, and peeked into the cruiser's wood-paneled forward cabin. There, sitting on the floor, was the king of Denmark.

Peter felt a flush of embarrassment to see his king in that kind of situation—almost as if he had seen him in his pajamas. But the king was tied at the wrists and ankles, with a red silk scarf around his mouth to keep him silent.

The king made no sound as Peter stepped inside. His eyes gave Peter a warm greeting, though, the same expression he had seen when they entered the king's study the first time they met.

"Is he in here?" Peter recognized Susanne's breathless voice from behind him. The boat was still rocking wildly as the boy scouts jumped around.

"Peter?" asked Elise.

Peter didn't answer. Before too many people could see him, he stepped over quickly to King Christian, untied the gag, then loosened the ropes that left red marks around the man's wrists. Out of respect, Peter lowered his eyes as he undid the last knot.

As soon as his mouth was free, King Christian flashed one of his broad smiles.

"Looks like you've been in the water, Master Peter." The king's voice came out hoarse and gravelly. "You look a little cleaner."

Peter looked down at the puddle under his feet. He had completely forgotten about being wet.

"Well, Peter," the king cleared his throat. "Perhaps you could help me get to my feet?"

There was another roar outside on the rear deck, and the boat rocked as police found their way on board.

"Where's King Christian?" asked one of the boys.

A minute later boys' faces appeared at all the portholes, looking in curiously as Peter, Elise, and Susanne helped the king to his feet.

"They carted me around like a box of pickled herring," King Christian told them, waving his hand at a large wooden box. Then he looked out curiously at the boys' faces and gave Peter and Elise a questioning look.

"Boy scouts," explained Peter. "They helped me chase you here, and they were the ones who stopped the boat. They jumped on the two German guys."

The king looked over at Susanne and raised his eyebrows.

"We didn't do anything," she explained, sounding as if she were apologizing. "Jens told us which direction to go, and we followed as best we could from the land."

"And who's the leader of this group of boys?" King Christian looked around once more. Mr. Lind stepped forward to the door, and King Christian shook his hand.

Mr. Lind cleared his throat. "Uh . . . I am . . . my name is Henning Lind, Your Majesty. We were just out for a little march before we left on a camp-out, sir. We just did what we could."

King Christian pumped Mr. Lind's hand. "You did more than that, Mr. Lind. You and your boys. These young people . . ."

He looked around at all the portholes again, at all the boys still following his moves. For a moment, Peter thought King Christian's eyes were filled with tears. But then Johanna piped up from the doorway.

"Do you remember me?" she asked in her little girl voice. The king looked straight at her and gave her a grin.

"Of course," he answered in German. "Johanna, is that right?"

Johanna beamed. "We caught the bad guys."

The king straightened up and took a step toward the stepladder that led up to the rear deck. "And a good thing, too."

A cheer went up when he stood straight on the deck, his arms around Peter on the right and Elise on the left. The police had already dragged Eyebrows up on shore and shut him away in the backseat of a black car.

"Long live King Christian!" shouted one of the scouts, and the crowd that had gathered around the waterfront echoed their own cheer. Police lights flashed in the early evening light. Up on the shore, Jens the stableboy still sat on Jubilee, smiling.

"The horse?" King Christian looked from Peter to Elise.

Elise looked over at the horse and rider. "It was the only way Jens could think of to chase you."

"Of course." The king nodded and raised his voice to be heard over all the noise, then waved at everyone who had crowded the old waterfront. In a moment a hush caught hold of everyone there. The policemen even turned off their sirens as the king struggled to make his way up to the shore. Then the king pointed at the police car where Eyebrows sat, staring straight ahead.

"Open that door," he commanded. "I want to see that man once more."

The police obeyed, opening the back door and pulling the handcuffed Eyebrows out of the car. He stood before the king, looking angry.

"And what do you have against me, young man?" asked King Christian, looking more stern than Peter had yet seen him. Eyebrows only looked over at Peter and ignored the king's question.

"We would have been long gone by now if it weren't for you. But at least you all fell for that oversized firecracker, just like we thought."

Peter kept a safe distance from the snarling man. "So it wasn't supposed to be a real bomb, then."

"Bomb?" He spat. "Not really a bomb. Just a little something to get people's attention while we grabbed your king here."

"But why?" Peter still wanted to know.

Eyebrows shrugged. "Those were our orders. General von Hanneken's last orders. That's how he wanted it done. And if we had the king, we thought maybe we could get a little cash out of the deal."

"Ransom," said the king, shaking his head in disgust.

"We knew it would be easy to grab the king," continued Eyebrows, "since he goes everywhere without bodyguards."

The crowd was hushed, and for a moment the king said nothing. Then he looked around and gestured at the crowd. "You're wrong, young man. These are my bodyguards."

With a nod from the king the police returned Eyebrows to the back of the police car and left. The king, looking weary, turned back to the stableboy on the royal horse.

"Jens, this has all been very exciting. But if you don't mind, I think I should like to ride Jubilee back home."

The king reached up to hold on to the saddle of the horse, then seemed to stumble.

"On second thought," he said, "you had better stay up there. And I'd better ride one of these police cars back to the palace."

THE KING'S PARADE

"Ooh," squealed Johanna, sitting straight up in the front seat of Susanne's little English convertible. "I've never been in a parade before."

"Well, wave, then," suggested Susanne. She turned to the twins and winked. "Don't tell her it's not a parade," she whispered.

Peter and Elise smiled and nodded. They sat on the back ledge of the little car, not really a backseat, with their feet wedged into the luggage space behind the only two seats in the convertible.

"Hang on," Elise told her brother with a smile. "You don't want to fall off the back end like you did your horse."

Peter laughed and looked around the street as the little convertible crawled along behind King Christian's car. "I don't think you need to worry about that," he told her.

No one told the boy scouts it wasn't a parade either. Just behind the king's car, they marched in their finest double-column formation, heads held high. Their drummer started up the beat once more, the same way he had when Peter had first run into them.

"The police have located your parents," Susanne told them, over her shoulder. "I spoke with them, and they're going to meet us back at the palace. But I'll tell you something, Peter. You look terrible."

Peter nodded with relief. "Yeah, I know. But are they all right?"

"Funny," Susanne laughed. "That's what they asked about you. Of course they're fine. After searching for you all day, though, I'd say they've been through a lot."

Elise nudged her brother. "Not that you haven't been through a lot, too, Peter."

"Me?" He tried to look casual but couldn't help smiling. "I hadn't thought about it."

"I'll bet you didn't." Elise smiled back at him.

In the corner of his eye Peter noticed someone leap out from the crowd that had gathered on the side of the busy street.

"Hey!" Peter shouted, whirling around. "You can't—"

A dark-haired teenager with hollow eyes ran toward them, his eye on the front seat. Peter could only think of swinging his legs around and jumping out. But his legs were stuck behind Johanna's seat.

"Johanna!" yelled the teenager, running up to the slowly moving car. Peter reached out to stop him, but Johanna was too quick.

"Gustav!" she squealed, almost jumping out of her seat. He plucked her out of the convertible before Peter could stop him as the little girl wrapped her arms around the boy's neck. "I knew you were here. I saw you in a big bus!"

Susanne put on the brakes, almost sending Peter and Elise tumbling. The twins stared first at what looked like a family reunion, then at each other.

"She wasn't kidding after all," Peter told his sister.

"I've been looking all over for you, little sister," replied the teenager, still holding Johanna in his arms. "My Danish friend Kai and his family have been trying to help me, but nobody could tell me where you were."

"Mama said you were dead." Johanna started to cry.

"I thought I was, too. But let's not talk about the war, little sister. I almost gave up finding you. Now, what are you doing? Who are these people?"

Susanne had been watching the whole scene with a puzzled smile, while Peter looked up ahead. All he could see was a wall of people following King Christian and the scouts.

Elise cleared her throat and introduced herself, then Peter. Gustav took their hands and nodded.

"I'm thankful you found my sister," he told them. "But I don't quite understand how."

"It's her brother," explained Elise, leaning over the seat to tell Susanne what was going on. "She thought he was dead and he's been looking for her."

Susanne nodded and smiled. "Oh, that's wonderful."

"Wait a minute." Peter tapped Elise on the shoulder while Johanna and her brother continued talking. "What did he say about someone helping him? Did he say Kai?"

"That's what he said. A lot of people are named Kai."

"Hey, um, Gustav?" Peter asked Johanna's brother.

Gustav looked a lot like his little sister, with blond hair and the same bright, dancing eyes. He looked like he still needed a few good meals, though. He perched Johanna back on the seat of the car and looked at Peter.

"Kai? Um, Pastor?" Peter fumbled for the right word in German, then turned to his sister. "Ask him, Elise."

Gustav searched the crowd around them as if he understood the question.

"Did someone mention my name?" came a booming voice from just behind them. Peter knew right then the answer to his question. Somehow, it was the same Kai.

Peter smiled as he turned around to meet his friend. "Pastor Kai, it *is* you!"

Pastor Kai laughed as he stepped up to their car. "I thought I lost Gustav. All of a sudden he saw something and started running. And now we run into you once more."

"Pastor Kai, my sister," reported Gustav, beaming.

"So that's what this is all about," answered Pastor Kai, getting a good look at Johanna and taking her hand. "*Guten tag*, Johanna. How do you do? Your brother has been dragging me all over this city, trying to find you. And now look who you're with."

"My friend, Pastor Kai," said Gustav. It sounded like those were the only words he knew in Danish. The friendly pastor patted Gustav on the back and smiled.

"This is going to take some explaining," said Peter. "Do we all know what's going on?"

"I think I'm starting to," replied Pastor Kai. "First this half-starved German boy turns up at my church for help in finding his sister. Says his parents were killed in the Dresden bombings, but his sister has been sent to someplace in Denmark by mistake. . . ."

"I don't think it was any mistake for us to find his sister at the Copenhagen train station," added Elise.

The tall pastor put his head back and laughed once more. "You're absolutely right, Elise. I can see this is one of those puzzles that only God could have put together. We're going to have to sit down and compare stories. We'll get your parents in on this, too."

"Only not here in the middle of the street," laughed Peter.

"Back to the palace!" suggested Susanne, starting up her car once more with a roar. The parade was long gone, but they only had another two blocks to go. Pastor Kai and Gustav kept up alongside the car, chatting as they went. Gustav still didn't seem to understand how his sister had been found by friends of the man who had been helping him in his own search.

"Does everyone know everyone else in this country?" he asked, scratching his head.

They all laughed when Elise had translated his question. And by then they were almost back at the palace.

"Uh-oh. Better watch out," Susanne warned them as they

rounded the last corner before the royal square. "Newspaper reporter dead ahead. If you want to duck down, now's your chance."

Peter looked over Susanne's head to see a young news reporter trotting their way. A policeman in the distance had pointed their car out to him. When he reached the car, he stood still for a moment in amazement and stared at the twins.

"You two again?" he asked them. It was the same photographer who had taken their picture when they were riding with King Christian on the two ponies.

The reporter looked to Susanne. "So what's all this about the king being kidnapped, Susanne? Can you tell me anything? No one would answer any questions except a crazy bunch of boy scouts."

Susanne pointed to the back of the car with her thumb. "You'd better ask them. These kids have the whole story."

"What do you know, kids?" The reporter took out his notebook as he trotted alongside the convertible. "Who can tell me what happened?"

Peter looked at his friends, shook his head in amazement, and smiled. "I guess I pretty much know the whole story. And I'll tell you one thing. It wasn't luck."

The reporter looked up from his notebook. Peter wondered how he could jog and write at the same time. "What do you mean?"

Peter smiled, sure of his answer this time. "Well, I always knew that God had everything under control. I just haven't been very good at telling people."

"You mean, like reporters?" asked the man, still keeping up.

"Yeah, like reporters. But King Christian was right. Only God could have taken care of Denmark. And He took care of us, too. Me and my sister, Elise. Little Johanna. Everybody."

A WHITE CROSS

"I like traveling in this boat better than Grandfather's row-boat, that's for sure." Elise tossed her hair in the cool ocean breeze as they watched the emerald green Danish coast slip slowly by. Peter's father and mother smiled as if they were enjoying the cruise.

"Aw, come on, Elise," said Peter, teasing his sister. "What does this boat have that ours doesn't?"

"Hot and cold running water, a motor, a kitchen with a real oven, a living room with couches, a deck to walk on, curtains . . ."

"Okay, okay, so our boat isn't quite the royal yacht."

Peter's father straightened up. "Well, kids, I never expected to get a ride on King Christian's little ship."

"Especially not a ride home to Helsingor," added Mrs. Andersen.

Peter just looked around in amazement. "Yeah, I know. It's like everything has been a dream since the chase yesterday. Too bad all the scouts couldn't come, too."

"They'll get their chance," said Elise. "Susanne said King

Christian is taking them on their own cruise next week to say thank you."

"But this is your turn," said their dad, beaming.

Pastor Kai opened the door to the deck and poked his head out. "Come on in, all you Andersens. I think the king is ready to start."

Feeling like a sailor, Peter tried not to hold on to the railing as the big, shiny motor yacht rose and fell to the gentle swells of the ocean. But he bumped into Elise as they all trooped into the main salon, or living room.

"Why don't you all sit down?" asked the king, who was sitting in a plush red overstuffed chair. "I've already found my favorite spot."

Queen Alexandrine was along this time, too, sitting quietly in a chair next to the king and smiling. Peter thought she looked more like a queen than King Christian looked like a king. Her silver hair was tucked up in a bun, and she was straight-backed and proper. Still, there was a hint of the same warm twinkle in her eye, and Peter liked the color of her regal blue dress.

Their friend Pastor Kai had been invited on this cruise, too, along with Johanna and her big brother. They all sat in a circle around the edge of the salon, along with Peter, Elise, and their parents. Susanne, dressed in a nautical blue-and-white striped skirt, slipped into the room from the steering area up forward and found a chair just as the king cleared his throat.

"I'm glad you could all come on this little cruise," he began, shifting around in his chair. "Because in all the excitement yesterday, with all the generals and guests at the palace, there really wasn't a chance to say what needed to be said."

Susanne smiled broadly, as if she knew some kind of secret.

"I . . . I owe you much more than just saying thank you," he continued, and the words seemed to catch in his throat. "I owe these two young people my life. So do a lot of other people, for that matter. General Eisenhower, the American general, wanted me to tell you how very grateful he was. He wanted to be here, but he had to catch an airplane back to the United States."

The king looked next at Johanna, who sat quietly by her brother, not knowing what was being said.

"Oh, I'm sorry. Johanna and her brother don't understand what we're saying." He looked straight at Johanna and her brother and switched over to a clear, slow German. "Johanna, I'm very grateful for what you did to help find the key. I'm also grateful to your bear for hiding it. I heard the story."

Peter tried not to giggle as Johanna looked back at the king and nodded seriously.

"I want you to keep the key and come back to visit us at the palace as often as you want. Will you do that?"

Johanna nodded again while her brother swallowed nervously.

"Gustav and I are going to stay at Pastor Kai's house," said Johanna, "but Elise promised she would come visit us there, too, right, Elise?"

"As much as Mom and Dad will let us," replied Elise. "I'm just glad you're back with your family. Your brother."

"Wait a minute," put in Mrs. Andersen. "I didn't catch all that German."

The king laughed. "Your daughter was making plans to visit Johanna at her new home already."

"Oh, I see." Mrs. Andersen stole a glance at her husband. "Well, I've been trying to talk Mr. Andersen into letting me visit my sister, now that the war is over. Maybe we can arrange something."

The king scratched his chin and looked around at his guests. "I don't mean to go on. And normally I would be wearing my formal uniform for such an occasion, instead of just a suit. But, Susanne, will you please get that box for me over on the counter?"

For a long moment all they could hear was the gentle humming of the engines and a seagull somewhere out behind them while the king opened a small white box.

"Normally these awards are only given to nobles, kings, and

generals." The king looked up with his twinkling eyes. "But for their bravery not only in the German submarine, but now also for saving the life of the king, two young people deserve to be honored with the Royal Danish Order of the Dannebro. This is one of the highest honors I can give."

Peter felt his knees knocking as the king pulled out first one, then two small white enamel crosses, each one on a red-edged white ribbon. The king held them up for all to see. Peter could make out the golden words on the cross: "God and the king."

"You two will be the youngest ever to receive such an award and join the order. But I think it's time. Come over here, please."

Elise and Peter held on to each other's arms as they slipped over to stand in front of the king. Queen Alexandrine helped her husband to his feet so that he could drape the crosses over first Elise's, then Peter's neck.

Peter stood there awkwardly, wondering if he should say anything.

"Look on the back," said King Christian. "I had it engraved with a special verse."

"What's it say, Peter?" asked Johanna, coming over to look at their awards. Susanne had draped a box camera around her neck and was looking down through the top of the box to take their picture. After a few adjustments, she held up her hand.

"Okay, you two, let's see a couple of smiles!"

The twins held their white crosses up to the light. When Peter tilted it to the side, he could barely make out the tiny lettering. He closed his eyes just as the camera's flash went off.

"Revelation three-seven," he whispered. "It says, Revelation three-seven."

"These are the words of him who is holy and true, who holds the key . . ." began the king.

" . . . and I know that you have little strength," finished Peter, "yet you have kept my word and have not denied my name."

EPILOGUE

No king was ever more dearly loved by the Danish people than King Christian the Tenth. His courage during the war kept the people hoping. His famous horse rides through the streets of the Danish capital brought them cheering. And his speeches pointed them toward better days ahead—as well as a higher calling on their lives.

He believed that God had a plan for the people of Denmark, if they would look to Him. He knew that God had saved their country through the long years of the Nazi invasion. He wasn't afraid to tell his country what he believed during his inspiring speeches. In a way, he was a light in the castle.

But of course not everyone admired the king. Denmark had enemies because the Danes refused to go along with the Nazi plan for Europe. And during the last days of the war, there were attempts on the king's life—even though he was never kidnapped.

There really was a secret tunnel built under the street in front of the palace, just as this story describes. While the king never had to use it, the Germans never discovered the hidden escape route.

There really were many refugees after the war, too. There's even a true story of a little German girl who was found at a Danish train station, lost and confused, until she was taken to live with a Danish family. The character of Johanna is based on that real little girl.

Unfortunately, there were many German families whose homes had been destroyed during the fighting. Jewish people whose country was torn apart. People whose houses had been blown up. Kids who were left without parents.

Some were sent to Denmark to stay for a while. They lived in camps until their families could be found or until there was a place for them back in their home countries.

Through it all, the Danes were very good at getting things back to normal, even when the world around them was at war. They loved their Tivoli Park in the middle of Copenhagen—one of Europe's best-known city amusement parks. And the boy scout troops in the city really did march down the streets on their way to camp-outs in the country. In Denmark, life would go on.

But the war had brought changes. The year 1945 was a time of new beginnings and new discoveries all across Europe—and families were looking for ways to make a fresh start. Before long, Peter and Elise would find themselves caught up in that wind of change.

———

Robert Elmer loves to hear from readers of THE YOUNG UNDERGROUND series. Write to him in care of the publisher:

Bethany House Publishers
11300 Hampshire Avenue South
Minneapolis, MN 55438